ARE WE EVER OUR OWN

Winner of the BOA Short Fiction Prize

ARE WE EVER OUR OWN

stories

Gabrielle Lucille Fuentes

American Reader Series No. 38

BOA Editions, Ltd.   Rochester, NY   2022

First Edition
22 23 24 25 7 6 5 4 3 2 1

For information about permission to reuse any material from this book, please
contact The Permissions Company at www.permissionscompany.com or e-mail
permdude@gmail.com.

Publications by BOA Editions, Ltd.—a not-for-profit corporation
under section 501 (c) (3) of the United States Internal Revenue
Code—are made possible with funds from a variety of sources,
including public funds from the Literature Program of the
National Endowment for the Arts; the New York State Council
on the Arts, a state agency; and the County of Monroe, NY.
Private funding sources the Max and Marian Farash Charitable
Foundation; the Mary S. Mulligan Charitable Trust; the
Rochester Area Community Foundation; the Steeple-Jack
Fund; the Ames-Amzalak Memorial Trust in memory of Henry Ames, Semon
Amzalak, and Dan Amzalak; the LGBT Fund of Greater Rochester; and contributions
from many individuals nationwide. See Colophon on page 220 for special individual
acknowledgments.

Cover Design: Sandy Knight
Interior Design and Composition: Richard Foerster
BOA Logo: Mirko

BOA Editions books are available electronically through BookShare, an online dis-
tributor offering Large-Print, Braille, Multimedia Audio Book, and Dyslexic formats,
as well as through e-readers that feature text to speech capabilities.

Library of Congress Cataloging-in-Publication Data
Names: Fuentes, Gabrielle Lucille, author.
Title: Are we ever our own : stories / Gabrielle Lucille Fuentes.
Description: First edition. | Rochester, NY : BOA Editions, Ltd., 2022. |
  Series: American reader series; no. 38 | Summary: "Gabrielle Lucille
  Fuentes's award-winning short story collection traces the Cuban diaspora through the
  struggles and triumphs of the Castell family's women"-- Provided by publisher.
Identifiers: LCCN 2021039144 (print) | LCCN 2021039145 (ebook) | ISBN
  9781950774616 (paperback) | ISBN 9781950774623 (ebook)
Subjects: LCGFT: Short stories.
Classification: LCC PS3606.U37 A88 2022 (print) | LCC PS3606.U37 (ebook)
  | DDC 813/.6--dc23
LC record available at https://lccn.loc.gov/2021039144
LC ebook record available at https://lccn.loc.gov/2021039145

BOA Editions, Ltd.
250 North Goodman Street, Suite 306
Rochester, NY 14607
www.boaeditions.org
A. Poulin, Jr., Founder (1938–1996)

para mi familia | for my family

CONTENTS

I. (el primer fantasma)

II. (begin again)

III. (el fantasma final)

I.

(el primer fantasma)

ANA MENDIETA HAUNTS THE BLOCK

Simon Marshall (interning tour guide, Art History, ABD) stands in the empty gravel yard of Donald Judd's museum in Marfa, Texas. The sun dips below the high walls of the compound, illuminating a perfect half of the courtyard. Behind Simon a wide expanse stretches, interrupted only by Donald's outdoor dining table, still holding two copper pots, as if the artist has just stepped inside to catch a phone call though he's been dead for decades. Simon, having shooed away the final tourist of the day, crosses the courtyard to lock the gates. They rear far above his head, solid wood aged to black and buttressed by iron. He feels medieval whenever he does this—who else but a feudal lord would need such protection? Tonight, there's a moment of resistance before the door shuts. A figure—shadowy, blurred around the edges—pushes through him, right through him.

At this moment he thinks not of Ana Mendieta, Cuban American visual and performance artist, enfant terrible of the 1980s New York art scene, who died far too young, her famous artist husband tried and acquitted for her murder. Simon doesn't know Ana yet, has never heard of her. Instead, he thinks of Caridad Armando-Mendoza, a Marfa High School senior who comes to the museum on Saturdays to help her aunt clean. Last week he walked in on her reading a bilingual edition of Sor Juana's poems

11

in the bathroom she was supposedly cleaning. He doesn't know why he thinks of Caridad, except that she's coming again tomorrow and he hasn't been able to not think of her all week.

Simon reaches for his phone, but it's still daylight, nothing to be afraid of. No crunch of gravel and nowhere in this purposefully bleak yard to hide. Instinctively, Simon creeps over to Donald's cement pool, edges sharp enough to crack a skull on, and gazes into the algae-dark water. But he gets there too early. The reflection of his face, backed by juniper bushes, rises to meet him. Nothing more. Ana has entered The Block, but she hasn't yet gone for a dip.

From September 8 to February 2, 20—, Ana Mendieta haunts Donald Judd's museum in Marfa, Texas. The Block consists of Donald's former studios, a monument to the minimalist artist, who is most famous for his reflective squares of polished steel and aluminum. The museum is on an old military compound, surrounded by a double layer of twelve-foot-high stucco walls and a gate it would take a battering ram to open. A footpath once ran between the studios, a shortcut from one end of town to the other. Donald put up the walls to stop that.

When visiting the museum, you enter the courtyard at a scheduled time, and the tour guide greets you and gives you instructions: no touching except for the outdoor furniture; absolutely no photos. Nothing, not the books or the stones set out on his desk, has been moved since Donald died. Part of the will. You enter the courtyard and gasp, because, yes, it is like the desert has been contained, in a space large enough to feel immense and small enough that it could be yours. Except it isn't.

Ana's first day here is an especially hot one. The tourists are sweating, and they keep reaching for the phones they surrendered at the gates. The heat is making them forgetful, making them irritable when they remember. After a dip in the pool, Ana stays out of everyone's way; her entrance the night before a little pushy, even for her. Instead, she makes to-do lists in the soft adobe of The Block's walls.

She'll move slowly, starting with the obvious. Just re-arranging one thing at a time, so only the tour guide will notice at first, then the small group of scholars who visit regularly. She'll start with Donald's grandfather's toy tops, because they are toys and meant to be played with. Time the spinning so that the tour group enters just when the tops are slowing down, wobbling like eggs on the massive table—perhaps they've caught a breeze. The next day, the group actually sees the tops start moving, one by one, faster and faster. Maybe they think it's a trick; maybe they believe the guide's explanation of a strong draft and a tilted table. Simon himself is beginning not to know what to believe.

Obviously, the library. All those books, and no one's read them since Donald kicked it. Probably not since long before. Start by messing with their order, organize them from worst artist to best. Then start removing them. Decide where they'll end up later.

Ana is unexpectedly pleased by Donald's studios. She has waited for decades to haunt them, worried it might seem a bit obvious, though Donald's connection to her husband was not a direct one. Mostly, she thought she'd be bored. But she loves the way there's nothing for the light to trip and catch on as it falls across the studio's cement floors, over the empty walls, to finally reach Donald's boxes, with their perfect lines and glossy surfaces. She sleeps inside a reflective red Plexiglas square, about the size of a large doghouse. Each night she thinks she won't return, but each morning, after a swim, she squeezes herself into the red square's unforgiving corners, jackknifing her curves to fit the angles. One afternoon, she wakes up laughing. Though her relationship to minimalism was fraught in life, in death, she loves it, or loves laughing at it, she can't tell which. Donald's side seems such a clean one: his art like blueprints for life, without the mess of bodies. As a ghost, she longs for this muted peace, though she can't understand what the living would want with it.

In each of Donald's studio/galleries is a bed with tucked-in white sheets and no headboard. He would nap in the afternoon, after looking at the already-made sculptures and scratching sketches for new ones. He paid people to build the sculptures off-site. In the galleries themselves: no equipment, no materials, no mess. After Ana finally tires of the red rectangle, she tries out each bed. The frames are a light, unvarnished wood—ur-Ikea—each bed pointed east. None of them are empty. Some of the ghostly occupants Ana seduces, some she is seduced by. Some she pushes into a corner, and they must watch while she undresses and musses the carefully-pressed covers. One ghost dives under the bed as soon as Ana touches the mattress and won't come back up. The sheets smell bitter; the pobrecita has probably been there for decades. Leave that bed alone.

It would be easy to do the haunting expected of her. But she paints no archetypal female silhouettes in menstrual red, doesn't fill the cavernous yard with the sound of a woman falling, a woman screaming for help, a woman hitting the ground. Doesn't carve her name across Donald's prized boxes. Sets fire to nothing. That's why she's here at The Block to begin with and not haunting Frank Stella's gallery (he posted her husband's $250,000 bail), or chasing her husband himself around his Berlin lofts. Sure, Donald and Frank were buddies, and Donald stood by her husband through the trial, but half the art world did too—split right down the middle and still fighting over it, over her. An encouraging thought.

The longer it takes for her identity to be revealed, the better. As soon as anyone knows who the ghost is, she can be written off. Man-hating from beyond the grave. Bra Burning Blah Blah Blah. Any named ghost's continued residence is no longer a haunting, but a corporation—all too corporeal. Patience is required of Ana. But she has about the same amount as when she was twenty-nine, trying to break into the New York art world, screaming that no one was looking, that nothing was moving fast enough.

In between tours, folded inside the red square or under the white covers, Ana wonders what kind of artist she would have become if she'd left her husband sooner or kept away from that open window. She was only just beginning, and if she is ever afraid, it is because she fears those who love her work love only the idea of it, love what it could have become: the unmade paintings, the unformed sculptures. The women who mourn her paint themselves red and pour fake blood on the steps of galleries that show her husband's work. They ask in huge hand-painted signs when a retrospective of his art goes up, *WHERE IS ANA MENDIETA? WHERE IS SHE?* She fears these women love only the possibility of her. Love her death more than her life. But it isn't so terrible, really, if those who love her art baptize themselves in her, sculpt and mold her work until it is more theirs than hers. Not so much to be afraid of.

After a few forays into ghostly rearrangement, Ana decides to focus on Donald's fans. They constitute the majority of each tour group, and they look so much alike. White men with carefully groomed beards, American heritage khakis, olive green T-shirts or fitted linen button-ups. No patterns, no bright colors. They all carry the same small notebooks, Japanese-made and logo-free, with black covers and neat grids on the pages. Some days when giving a tour, Simon pretends he's not a Judd scholar, just to see how long it takes one of the fans to start lecturing in his place. While one orates, the others caress the harsh angles of Donald's heavy wooden patio sets even more lovingly, as if their touches could make up for the fact that this supposed guide, someone who does not truly understand Donald's work, gets to spend so much time around it.

Ana laughs at these men, but she likes them too, especially en masse. They look like warehouse inventory, carefully stacked, ready for use. She transposes the veiny forearms of one onto another with a black beard down to his chest. Chops off his man bun, preferring something more clean-cut, if you're gonna have all that beard. Then, or perhaps concurrently with imagining what positions the reconstructed fans might take over or under her, she enters each of them and sets off a little cause and effect in their circuitry. Beneath the Texas sun, the men stop genuflecting to the furniture. They turn to each other and whisper their deepest fear and dearest wish. They begin undressing each other, slowly, taking time to admire both their fine linen shirts and the curls of hair sprouting around nipple and navel. Naked, they kneel and roll in the gravel. They realize their knees have turned to lips, their fingers and heels too. Their skin colored in dust and spit, a myriad of baroque patterns. Ana doesn't want to turn away, but she does. She's wasted enough time on men who thought they were gods.

It is then, after her first series of possessions (also her

last, too successful to repeat), that Ana finally spots Caridad Armando-Mendoza. Hidden behind the juniper bushes in the courtyard, watching the naked men roll around in the dirt, Caridad is doubled over in laughter.

On Saturdays, Paula, Caridad's aunt, cleans The Block—not the sculptures, you practically need special degrees to do that, but the floors, the shelves, the bathrooms. At first Ana's presence causes Paula to retreat, draw in on herself and tighten her sweatshirt hood, as if against a sudden November wind. But Ana quickly makes it clear that she is not haunting Paula, and Paula relaxes. Even so, on the afternoons Caridad comes to help, Paula steers her teenage niece away from the rooms she thinks Ana might be in, shooing her from building to building, using Caridad's admitted lack of skills as an excuse to move her along. Paula doesn't get paid by the hour, but in a lump sum, and her duties at The Block cut into her Saturday night bingo game.

While dusting the library one week, Caridad pulls a book from the shelf. She instantly feels, instead of the huge hand of an anonymous boss swooping down, a presence (Ana's) buzzing warmly beside her. She pulls another book and the buzzing is fiercer, like her girlfriends are surrounding her, clapping and whooping, but she's alone and there's no sound. More books, their covers heavy, their pages glossy with expensive color images. Caridad rushes through cleaning the bathroom, drags a space heater inside, rolls her jean jacket into a cushion for the hard toilet seat, and reads all afternoon.

Paula knows what Caridad is up to, but Caridad is the one everyone in the family is working for, the one they've chosen to be The One who'll get out. Caridad's mom was supposed to be that one, until, well, Caridad, and Paula's decided it's up to her to make sure that this time the choice sticks. Caridad glides through her days—as much as she can in the still-segregated Texas town. No one complains about her reading at the dinner table or going to Drama Club and Yearbook Club or founding her school's LGBTQIA Alliance when the other daughters her age are at home taking care of their siblings. No one collects her library fines (another aunt is a volunteer librarian) or busts her for smoking, despite the Armando-Mendoza's propensity for lung cancer. Caridad's aware of the pressure on her, she thinks she's got everyone fooled with the bathroom reading and clove cigarettes. But her cousins have all agreed: that's the worst she'll get her hands on until she gets her ass to college. God help her if she fucks up then. Then she's on her own.

Paula explains all this to Ana. While she's cleaning, Paula often calls her cousin in Houston to catch up on family gossip, speaking quietly into the headset Caridad gave her. When Paula speaks to Ana, it looks the same as if she were talking on the phone—a woman moving slowly through an open room, carrying on a conversation with no one you can see.

Paula doesn't know Ana's history, but she can sense a brokenness in her, one that wants to keep splintering. She doesn't know about Ana's fall, but she can smell too much wine and air moving over a body the way it does when that's the last thing a body feels before a hard and ending ground. She's never been to New York, but can smell the city's morgue.

Paula speaks to Ana in part to keep Ana on her toes and in part because Caridad's future is weighing on her and in part because she likes Ana, though she can't understand why she doesn't haunt somewhere comfier and surrounded by her own people. Paula likes Ana for the same reasons she can't trust her. Nothing more dangerous than a lone Cuban, Paula says. You people need your people. She figures Ana would know that the Armando-Mendozas are Cuban themselves: the paternal branch of an island clan that fled to Mexico a century ago and slowly made their way north, dropping possessions and surnames on the way.

While Caridad is in the bathroom reading about Late Abstract Expressionism and Land Art, Ana and Paula discuss the works around them. Paula likes the narrow blue plastic rectangles stacked on the wall, like a ladder without supports. She likes that they tell a story, and Ana says they don't have to, and Paula says, Well, I don't have to clean very well; those fools wouldn't notice. Paula says, I like to think about climbing that blue ladder and why I would be climbing and where I'd go. She likes how she feels she's outside in the studios even though she's inside. That's cheating, though. Grabbing so much space for yourself, and why not just be outside? Paula agrees with Ana that it's the peace of death at The Block. But it's white people's death. No big party, no sendoff: quiet and restrained. At The Block there's space enough for a giant, but it doesn't make me feel small. Just angry.

Can Caridad see Ana? She thinks something is there. A palindromic gaze? At first Caridad had felt watched and she hid in the bathroom, worried someone—the tour guide Simon, his boss, a tourist—was following her. But the feeling shifted when she pulled that book from the shelf. *Someone* was by her side. It didn't feel like a really famous someone—Our Lady of Guadalupe or her namesake La Caridad del Cobre—someone smaller, La Juquilita maybe. Someone who had enough of an opening in their schedule to keep the dirt Caridad just swept up from getting caught in a passing draft, someone tapping on her shoulder right before Simon rounded the corner and caught her drawing hearts with her finger-smudge on one of Donald's shiny rectangles. Caridad leans back, catches her reflection on the metal instead.

Caridad doesn't ask Ana how she died; she would never be so rude. But she too can see falling all around Ana, a body suspended, about to unravel. Ana exits the gallery, floats up, floats out, but Caridad has enough. She knows that though Ana took photos of the impressions her body made in snow, sand, mud, grass, took photos of her impact on this earth for years, when the police arrived and found her body, they took none. The police believed her husband's account of suicide brought on by a fiery island temper and uncontrollable jealousy. Though the photos would probably have been important in the trial, a part of Ana is glad that the final images of her are not something she had no control over, glad that the last photos of her body are ones she herself staged.

Caridad asks Ana about her art and life instead. Ana and her sister left Cuba alone as kids. For years, they floated between foster homes and orphanages. In college in Iowa, Ana started her *Silueta* series, pressing her body into the surfaces around her, reaching for the ground she'd lost, documenting that reach. She folded herself into riverbanks, bought flowers and covered her body into a living grave, later etched female figures in sand and painted them with red dye or filled them with gunpowder and set them on fire. Meaning in making, not remaining. The brief outline of her body, the dirt forgetting her. Caridad asks, What did it feel like to stretch yourself into the snow, to lie naked in a field over a skeleton? Were you thinking about how best to capture the performance, the angles to shoot from, or did you disappear, for a moment, into the earth?

Caridad and Ana discuss their plans for The Block. Not so much in words as in actions and their reactions. Caridad doesn't place the books she reads back on the shelves, but sticks them inside the rectangle where Ana spends most of her nights. The sculpture plays with reflections—you can never see yourself, just whatever's occurring on the other side. Caridad reaches her hand into the warm, red glow, and the books disappear. She places her local library card on top of a pile. Caridad trusts Ana will know what to do.

It takes the tour guide Simon years to confirm that the figure who pushed through him as he closed the gates, and who left, months later, wrapped like a stole around two Dutch tourists, was Ana. He stumbles on her work much later, when he's almost forgotten what Caridad actually looked like reading in the bathroom, but not the shame that shrouds that image. When he eventually sees one of Ana's self-portraits on a poorly-lit museum wall, he recognizes her immediately, even though she's sporting sideburns and a pasted-on handlebar mustache that she trimmed off a friend's beard. Looking at her photos—documents of performances, assumed identities—Simon thinks that the impression Ana leaves of her body on mud, on glass, on his tongue still all these years later, is difficult to name. Form yet formless. The photos document the attempt to capture the fragile and fading, turning every muddy riverbank into a place to rest, sink, curse. He sees Ana's photos and he can finally name the hunger he felt staring at Donald's perfect boxes day after day. He had longed for something that could slip away and still be remembered. Something that left just a taste of itself.

Simon notices the changes at The Block. At first, he does nothing. He suspects Caridad is behind it, but he's been reading Marx and he doesn't want to be a bourgeois sellout and there's that other, more embarrassing reason. When the books go missing, he ignores that too, thinking of Caridad's laugh when the Donald wannabes rolled in the dirt. But when almost half the library is gone, he knows that he has to do something or else he'll be fired and reprimanded and cast into the utter darkness of a grad student without reliable references or postdoc prospects.

He corners Caridad in one of the smaller galleries. He doesn't mean to, but still he does.

At first he talks about continental philosophy, and then he talks about his job and his parents and how there isn't anything green in Marfa, not like where he's from, in Oregon, and how he's on her side, but maybe she's just gone a little too far, and that he really needs this job because he needs where this job will lead, the job after this job, that's what he needs, and then he talks about Caridad herself, what he thinks about her, what he's decided about her, which is more accurately a cloaked description of what he *feels* about her, but he doesn't say that, surely, doesn't go that far, doesn't make that much of a fool, and Caridad kind of nods slowly and manages to step around him, and he shouts after her and she tries to play it cool—shrugs and waves. His boss is in Berlin at a conference and hasn't been answering emails. The books keep disappearing, and what if it's not just the books, what if something else disappears next, something big, something priceless, and it's Simon, Simon who will be blamed? He shouts again after Caridad, but she's already across the courtyard. She's not listening; she's probably laughing. Not knowing what else to do and having been taught his whole life to do it, Simon calls the cops.

He regrets it immediately, but still he does.

When Caridad tells the story of The Block and Ana to her first-year college roommates and then later in other forms (visual, written), she keeps her role to a minimum. She describes Ana not as she experienced her—a devilish saint by her side—but as she found her in her art, first in tiny pictures on her phone and then in books in her university library. (It made Donald's seem so small.) Ana with her black hair parted down the middle and tied in a ponytail at the base of her neck. Dark, unplucked eyebrows, and clothes that seemed at first upsettingly nondescript. Jeans and crew-neck T-shirts. No Frida skirts or bangles, no embroidered blouses or flowers in her hair. Cubans don't have all that, Paula told her. That's one of the reasons we're such pains in the ass.

The boring clothes bothered Caridad, until she started thinking about other things. The quality of fixative necessary to congeal gravel. Easily producible and portable abrasives for metal, plastic, glass. A substance that could burn without spreading. How to enter museums and galleries without being noticed.

When she tells the story in her dorm room, she tells how Paula was fired (since Caridad herself wasn't on the payroll) even though the books reappeared *while* they were being questioned by the police and faster than any person could have carried them in. She describes Simon's emails, how many times he apologized (seventeen), how many times she answered (zero). The news of the disappearing and reappearing books made the local paper. Though Paula was rehired, the town's rival Judd museum saw the article and made a better offer. The one and only instance Paula could point to of white people's infighting benefiting anyone else.

What Caridad doesn't talk about, not for years, are those final moments at The Block. She left Simon to his shouting and went back to cleaning the bathroom. Swept the floors, wiped down the sink, finished by polishing the mirror, not with an old T-shirt sprayed with vinegar as Paula taught her, but with her own breath. Through the open window, she heard tires on the gravel road outside The Block and police radios clicking, counted the seconds to their arrival. Caridad thought of the final haunt then, in her last moments at The Block, the haunt that hadn't happened yet, the haunt no one would forget. She felt that buzzing grow, swelling in the tiny room, heat hazing the mirror. The fog cleared, and she locked eyes with the sole figure who emerged from the glass.

Paula is ready to help with the final haunt. Ana has flown by then, but Paula and Caridad feel the protective umbrella of double jeopardy. Who will suspect them now that they have been proven incapable of whatever occurred? And no one wants to think too hard about what did occur, about just how it could have been possible.

Their work is slow. It starts at the end of spring and takes the rest of the summer. In the days before Caridad leaves, Paula, Caridad, and Paula's bingo team circle the town at night, digging into the sand with thin, pointed shovels, not too deep, no pattern that could be noticed standing nearby. On Caridad's final night in Marfa, Paula sets the path they've made aglow, and the whole town is wrapped in the warm, red light. There's no danger of it spreading; Caridad's seen to that. The light feels—depending on who you are, whether you want to leave or stay, whether you build walls to protect your creations or let people walk through them—like a welcome embrace or an all-consuming fire.

The next morning, as many of Caridad's family who can, pack into Paula's car to make the drive to Austin. The car is full, but it's early, the sun just coming up over the mountains, and everyone is silent. Caridad looks back one last time, and it is as she and Paula planned. From the top of the hill, you can see the scorched silhouette of a woman: huge, visible in whole only when leaving. Caridad will speak of this moment years later. Her first work, though she will never call it hers alone.

II.

(begin again)

THE BURIAL OF FIDELIA ARMANDO CASTELL

1.

In those days, the houses were built with courtyards slicing out their centers. Only a few square meters at the bottom, a careful extraction that allowed light and air to filter through every level. *In those days*, I say, though the events of this story occurred long after La Pieza—our dear city perched on the southern tip of a narrow island, bordered by thick jungle and choppy sea—had begun to diminish. Long after La Pieza's grand mansions had been divided into separate apartments and separate families, families who became, despite their different names, closer than kin. In partitioned houses, the courtyard was even more important. The interior-facing balconies were the only clean and airy place for those families who shared floors and staircases, who divided their rooms with each new generation. In this time, the time of this story, a time that is also long ago, a building was known by its courtyard. Its residents' reputation—and their likelihood of surviving the war and interminable occupation—were judged by that slice of air, by the small open heart at the house's base.

At 147 de la Concha, the housekeeper—who owned no part of the building, but carried the keys and knew its history and divisions better than anyone—lived on the first floor. Though she had no balcony and everyone who lived above her walked through the courtyard—*her* only open space—she was paid for the intrusion with information she gathered and the power she held in the residents' lives. Doña Alba of 147 de la Concha was a kind tyrant, beloved by all who passed her tiny, arched door. She knew the secrets of each family and was called into their apartments to mediate disagreements or to provide the true account of events long past or passed in the night when only she could hear them. But there was one purpose, of the many to which she devoted her considerable power, that she held above all others: the preservation of young girls' honor. For this reason, no matter the time or weather, Doña Alba could be found watering her plants or sweeping the dirt floor of the courtyard whenever Fidelia Armando Castell or Rosa Agüero Gijón came out on their balconies.

The residence of 147 de la Concha held two families and their extensions: the Armando Castells and the Agüero Gijóns. Though each family was prominent, neither were wealthy, so the courtyard had a dirt rather than tile floor. There's nothing cleaner than a dirt floor, Doña Alba said, at least once a week. She preferred earth that allowed her to water her hibiscus and mint without wondering where the water would go, and she did not have to spend extra time on her knees scrubbing tile. The residents not only agreed, but held that the dirt marked their building as more prestigious. The newer buildings, with tile or those awful cement stones that burned children's bare feet and palms, had been built *after* the struggle for independence, whereas 147 de la Concha had been built *before*. Under the occupation, that long-ago war was remembered rather quaintly. The starvation campaigns; the camps where thousands died; the independence fighters who freed themselves from enslavement, started the rebellion, and won the war: all cast in a false, rosy glow. Despite the old enemy's barbarity, we whispered, at least we shared the same language, a beautiful tongue we could all agree on. Under the occupation, the enemy spoke words we could not understand, clotted sounds that shared few roots with our own.

147 de la Concha's courtyard was mostly covered by Doña Alba's flowers and herbs and the large rocker which she scooted across the floor depending on the balcony the residents she was talking with or spying on stood. Between Doña Alba's sweeping and sprinkling water, and the residents' footsteps packing the dirt for decades, the courtyard floor was harder than marble. No heel could make a mark. Any shovel would have bent like a blade of grass trying to scuff a diamond.

Even the shoes of Fidelia Armando Castell, called Fidé, whose once-respectable kitten heels she had heightened with pieces of wood and whittled to points that stuck in the cobblestones and sidewalk grates outside the plaza, even these did not leave a dent deeper than a pigeon-print in the dirt. Her heels were the reason, Doña Alba lamented later, that it took her so long to know what the girl was up to. Fidelia left no trace, not a whisper. Only the ceiba tree, which had entered the building in a pot before Fidelia was born and now took up an entire corner of the courtyard, had been able to make its mark on the dirt floor. Years ago, Doña Alba's (now) late husband, had seen the ceiba struggling. He had cracked the pot and extracted the clay shards from the roots, allowing the tree to expand into the heretofore impenetrable dirt.

Until Fidelia's escapes, Doña Alba's reign over the courtyard was firm. She argued that even if her control *appeared* to waver, she was only allowing those she had trained to step forward into their sacred duties. One such example she often repeated was a story of Fidelia Armando Castell and Rosa Agüero Gijón together in the courtyard, when they were still small enough to hide behind the pots of herbs, yet too fast for Doña Alba to catch, a story from long before the occupation. Back then, long ago, with their backs turned, only the color of the little girls' braids (Fidelia's dark brown mixed with red and tightly curled, Rosa's black and oiled straight), kept them from being twins. Their bodies were the same disproportions: long legs, short torsos, big knees, sprawling hands that Rosa grew into, but Fidelia did not. Rosa had a fine black mustache that stood out on her skin, though she didn't know she had it yet. Their features were different, yes, but their expressions and movements were the same, having been each other's mirror since Fidelia was old enough to reach through the balcony bars and wave at the little girl across the courtyard.

In their play, other children crowded around them—cousins and neighbors, on the balconies, passing through the courtyard—but to Fidelia and Rosa, no one else existed. Their fantasies could take months to unfold, with intricate yet mutable plots that enabled them to be beasts and ladies and the personification of different land formations or even shifts in the weather.

One afternoon, a girl who lived on the wealthy side of Calle de la Concha, twice as tall as either of them for being raised on both yuca and fine steaks, asked to join in their play. The girl was ignored. She asked again. She was ignored again. The third time she asked and heard not even a word in response, this tall, rich girl grabbed Fidelia by the arm and threw her to the ground. Rosa leapt up and charged, head down, but the girl knew how to fight and dodged her easily. The bully girl went straight again for Fidelia, who couldn't even stand up so great was the whiplash from her fantasy struggle to this real one. She could only cover her face with her hands and wail. Rosa lunged at the big girl again and kicked and pulled her dress, but the girl had found the pair's underbelly. The girl yanked Fidelia's braids and spit on her pinafore, hammering her with scrubby fists, until there was a shout—a squawk really, like a hen or crow—from the balcony above. The big girl looked up at Elmo, Rosa's youngest brother who, though he was only two years younger than Rosa and eighteen months younger than Fidelia, was still too young to play in the courtyard. Elmo squawked again, then pulled down his short pants and pissed all over the girl. So perfect was his aim that not a drop landed on Rosa and Fidelia, who, hearing him, had the good sense to run to the other side of the courtyard. Rosa shouted in triumph—a sound not too different from her brother's—and raised her fists in the air, holding them there, a tiny statue of militant joy. Fidelia, however, was silent. Her eyes darted between Elmo and the intruder. The girl, stunned and still dripping, slunk from the courtyard.

Seeing her walk away, Rosa and Fidelia started laughing. It took them days to stop. Even years later, spotting the girl—who had grown up to be boring, respectable, and without an ounce of style—would send them into fits. Fidelia would sniff exaggeratedly or Rosa would raise her handkerchief to her nose and arch her eyebrows and they would have to run back to 147 de la Concha they were laughing so hard. Then Doña Alba would chase them with her dust cloths for showing their teeth and arching their necks in public, because who might follow them home after such a display? She could only be calmed when reminded that she kept a careful watch on the courtyard and had trained all the boys in the building to do the same. Doña Alba would sit in her rocker, both girls cooling her face with her sandalwood fans, and say yes, she had trained the boys well, and a good thing too, considering all that the girls—their white teeth, long necks—would need protecting from.

After the intruder girl had run away, both Fidelia and Rosa gave Elmo the sweets they had saved from Carnival the month before. Elmo ate them all at once: the honeyed cake of the capuchinos now dry, the marzipan with a crust of iron around their still-soft centers. He threw up on the balcony, and Rosa and Fidelia started laughing again.

"Poor baby," Fidelia said when she could speak. "Poor baby Elmo, you saved us."

2.

Fidelia's family (the Armando Castells), were a haberdasher branch of a clan that stretched across not only our little island, but all the others in the greater archipelago. Rosa's (the Agüero Gijóns) had lived in the city for as long as anyone could remember. The families were proudly mestizo, tracing their complicated kinship to both the independence fighters and the men who believed they had owned them, and even further back, to the time when Our Lady of Charity rose out of the sea to save three little boys about to be dashed by waves.

But neither Rosa nor Fidelia cared much about this history, about the dusty pamphlets on the laws of physiognomy that once lay decaying in the back drawers of ancient pharmacies and now, since the occupation, had begun to resurface. Rosa knew only that in the years since the occupation, her world had shrunk. Fewer dresses, fewer streets she could walk on, fewer custards and translations of French novels, fewer hours she could walk those fewer streets. And her world kept shrinking. Her dresses down to two, one to wash and one to wear, and then only one so at the end of the week she had to wait, watching her dress dry on the balcony railing, stuck behind the latticed shutters, not even able to peek her head far enough out to see the drops of water land on the dirt courtyard below, waiting for Fidelia to return from wherever she'd snuck off to. Because by then Fidelia Armando Castell was nineteen, and there were few powers—not even Doña Alba's—that could have stopped her from slipping out of 147 de la Concha and finding someone to wrap his arm around her waist while music played.

On each block, on each night since the occupation began—which was an eternity for Fidelia, as long as Elmo (seventeen) had considered himself a man, and certainly longer than anyone younger than little Mirian (Fidelia's youngest sister) could actually remember—there had been the young people's dances. They were held in the courtyards of the larger residences, the ones with tile floors or not so many plants (certainly no overgrown ceibas) or with a building plan that allowed entry to the upper balconies without having to cross through each apartment. Even overseen by the housekeepers and older family members, these parties were riotous. The bands played all night, far longer than they'd been paid to, and the young people danced as long as there was music. The old people never complained that these parties occurred with a frequency and frenzy unheard of in their youth. They did not do what every generation does once its feet hurt too much to dance until dawn. They understood the dances were necessary.

For a time, the young people's parties followed a certain pattern. Each day, the group of girls who would host set about decorating their courtyard with birds of paradise gathered beside the cliffs, bits of colored paper from old advertisements cut into stars and moons, anything they could scavenge from the tin man or their closets. By evening they had constructed their costumes, made of the same set of materials and shaped according to the theme of the night. The themes began light-heartedly, extensions of secondary school balls: *Land of the Fairies* with paper wings and flower coronets (both Rosa and Fidelia participated); *Beneath the Sea*, with conch shell tops over their dresses and skirts woven of seaweed with long tails, a hint towards risqué, yet still innocent (Fidelia attended, but by this time Rosa was no longer allowed outside after dark). At a certain point the themes began to twist, to torque and complicate, until they culminated in the infamous *Ripeness Is Only the Onset of Decay*. On that night, the girls wore elaborate headdresses of wilted carrot tops, pineapple heads, and onion skins. They picked the worst of the rags from the tin man and—like the unraveling mummy that had toured the island years ago—wrapped themselves tightly in strips of fabric, allowing shards of skin to show at the midriffs and thighs. They looked beautiful until you got close. By morning the courtyard sloshed with fetid vegetables. Everyone stank from sweat, from the garbage-stained rags, from the rotten tomatoes the girls had smeared on the walls late in the night. The lead girl, who wore two boiled-to-almost-collapsing pig's feet woven into a wreath above her head like horns, drank the final drag of cane liquor and cried out, "The stench is the point." They lived, she continued, invaded and occupied by the most putrid stink, and no dance or costume, no *party* was going to change that. The courtyard was almost empty, the band packing up, the morning coming slow and soft like the girl's heartbeat had once been long ago in a time she could not really remember. "And," she shouted to the pigeons and the pink dawn clouds, "I will never forget it! I will never forget the stink!"

She disappeared three days later and the themed parties stopped. In their place, the local boys concocted elaborate competitions, combinations of skill and chance with each point or deduction payable in a shot of cane liquor. Rosa's brother Elmo was at every party, quietly leading the revelers though not drinking much himself, because, since the games were often his own creation, they were too easy for him to win. And Elmo was always looking for Fidelia, who was always there until she was not, and even when she was there he would only be able to stand by her while looking up at the stars until someone pushed his way between them and asked her to dance. Before the moon set, Elmo, along with everyone else, had forgotten again about the girl in her pig's-foot crown crying to the dawn. Instead, he was thinking of a memory he didn't quite possess, but that had been told to him so many times he almost remembered it. It was from long before the occupation, when Rosa and Fidelia were still small enough to hide behind the pots of herbs and too fast for Doña Alba to catch. He could just remember—if he pasted words and images borrowed from other moments together to fit—the acrid taste of the sweets coming up his throat, the shape of Fidelia's palm on his back, the sound of her laughter, the joy that he had in protecting her.

Whether due to the courtyard dirt's silence or Doña Alba's advancing age, no one knew when Fidelia stopped going with her neighborhood friends to the young people's parties and started going alone to the dance halls ringed round the Plaza Mayor. These dance halls teemed, in the words of the pig's-foot girl, like an overflowing outhouse. There were soldiers, bureaucrats, officers, all the occupation's necessary detritus, celebrating each night their presence in a city that had long ago stopped fighting. No one knew Fidelia had joined them, danced among them—the enemy, the occupiers—twirling in her whittled heels, no one but Rosa.

By the time Fidelia started going to the dance halls, Rosa's world had shrunk to the size of 147 de la Concha's courtyard. That summer, her father had forbidden her from leaving the house in the evening. By fall, he would not let her leave the house at all, even with Elmo as escort. The city had begun to turn, first under the pressure of the invading forces and later through a motivation all its own. In their home, the windows facing the street were kept closed. Rafael Agüero entered at dawn and returned at dusk. Though the patriarch of the Armando Castells was less strict, Rafael Agüero's family (perhaps the wiser of the two) had decided that only he was allowed to leave 147 de la Concha. His grown sons across the balcony with families of their own made their own decisions, but they soon mirrored their father's. Rosa's youngest sister Bernicia watched Rosa all day, saw Rosa growing more and more silent. Each night, Elmo argued with his father that he wanted to go out, to the dances or just walk up and down the Malecón. It made him less of a man to not be trusted to leave and return, to take care of himself. He would shout and pound his fist on the table, apologize to his mother, and leave, with the instructions for that night's drinking game crumpled in his hand. Rafael tried to stay awake to wait for him.

Of course, Rosa knew where Fidelia went. She knew days and even weeks before Fidelia's first venture; had asked to hear, again and again, her friend's plots to sneak down Peñitas and Calixto and enter the dance halls. Begged Fidelia to tell her, in descriptions whose durations mirrored the living of them, what she saw when she finally entered. In a whisper, Fidelia described the way the lights sparkled through the bottles of ersatz champagne—which even she knew was fake, though she didn't care—how the lights made the singer's dress look like flames. How the singer was always about to be swallowed up, not by the lights or the strength of her voice, but by the eyes of everyone in the hall watching. It was only because the attention was never quite complete that the singer stayed alive long enough to finish her song.

In the day's heat, the shutters closed to keep out the sun, breeze, and prying eyes, Fidelia whispered to Rosa. In the moment before Fidelia spoke, her hands cupped over Rosa's ear like over a shell, both friends remembered their childhood games, when they were small enough to hide behind the herbs in the courtyard and too fast for Doña Alba to catch. They didn't laugh when they remembered the bully girl and Elmo's perfect arc of urine, but they remembered laughing and remembered being both afraid and amazed. The memory linked them as much as the words Fidelia shaped as they lay on the thin mattress Rosa had been born on, curled around each other, two *c*'s facing and linked, Fidelia speaking and Rosa listening. If Rosa's sisters tried to listen too, Rosa kicked at them. When the younger girls retreated, Rosa and Fidelia let their feet dangle off the bed, toes curling and uncurling in the empty space between the mattress frame and the floor. Rosa asked Fidelia to elaborate and Fidelia would. Soon Rosa hardly needed to ask, she said just enough to keep Fidelia speaking and could lie for hours, carried away on Fidelia's voice.

3.

What next?

Fidelia must go again to the dances and this time Rosa must go too. Then must come the dance hall itself with lights sparkling through fake champagne as Fidelia promised and the singer alight, but not engulfed. Then must come the officers and soldiers and translators and telegraph men, and Rosa hated them because they were the invaders, the occupiers, the reason her mother made coffee that was half chickpea flour and clogged the espresso pot and made it explode and cut Elmo right under his eye. Almost blinded him. Hated them for the ration stamps and rice with moths and the girl haloed in pig's feet, hated them until a telegraph man complimented her dress, which was Fidelia's, but that even Fidelia admitted looked better on her, and a lieutenant pulled out a chair for her, and another ordered a glass of fizzy wine or cava or whatever it was that sparked in her mouth like those tiny paper parcels of gunpowder children throw on stone doorways to hear them pop. Then must come what Fidelia did or did not do and what the lieutenant and the telegraph officer did most certainly do. And after that.

But first the dancing and Rosa's discovery that she could dance, to any music, and so well that it became a challenge the whole hall seemed to be in on: to ask the singer, imported from the capital, to play the newest songs, the oldest songs, the fastest songs. And that it was not the bubbling drinks or the tablecloths pressed as her grandmother used to press them or even the compliments, but that she, Rosa, was taking up a space large enough to be offered a chair, had a body that could consume a whole glass and ask for another, limbs that could fill in the layers of organza that made up Fidelia's dress. Her life had been: sitting in her apartment in the dark all day, sharing the bed with her sisters who pinched and snored and stole the blankets, rotating the wearing of the one dress not too tatty to appear out on the inner balcony. When not wearing that dress, she sat in the shadows cast by the shutters, sucking on a licorice root, gnawing until the stick was a soggy pith, until even her throat was numb. Waiting. Waiting for nothing except Fidelia to come home from the dances, pretend to sleep, and then to creep, on the pretense of a neighborly errand, to tell Rosa all she had done the night before. Sitting and waiting and looking over the courtyard in her nightgown so old it shone, Rosa had begun to believe she did not exist. She did not eat enough for a whole stomach. She did not speak enough for a whole mouth. She was being worn into a thin sliver, a lozenge disappearing on a child's tongue. The very little that was left was sustained by Fidelia's whispers. But that very little had been feeding on those words so long it was nothing without them. Rosa had listened to Fidelia's stories until she felt she would devour her friend. Her hunger shaped into a thick cloud, smelling like the inside of an animal's den, musky and slightly furred. This cloud swelled out of her pores that could do nothing but stain and stain again that hated old nightgown. Even the cloud was not her. Even my hunger is not my own, and since it's all I have, I am gone.

But she was not. Rosa looked at the men in the dance hall, some in uniform and some in fine suits, and they looked back at her. In their faces, she saw herself. Not what she looked like, but that she could be looked at. Further proof: their hands did not clasp around emptiness, but around another hand, solid enough to pulse back against their palms. They did not walk to the dance floor to dance alone. They waited until the song was over and swept through the crowd to ask for the next dance, not from a slice of empty air, but from a body, whole and glowing in sweat that creased her gloves, breath passing lips that marked her glass with a stain.

It must be remembered that the men who raped her tore and battered at someone newly born to herself. Someone still blinking in the light of her shockingly solid reflection. The names they whispered, all the usual ones, they cursed into ears still wet and unfolding. Ears newly wrung from the tunnel of the dance floor, reborn just moments before.

When the men were done, Fidelia, who had two dances ago noticed Rosa missing, but had only just started looking, opened a side door leading to the alley where she knew the soldiers often smoked or necked. For a moment, she thought she saw herself in Rosa's place, against the stucco wall. For it was Fidelia who had brought Rosa to the dance hall, so why shouldn't it be Fidelia, face framed by the light through the doorway, uncovering this unwatchable aftermath, and not Rosa? Rosa, her mirror and memory, the same as her in every way.

But before all that, there is Rosa and Fidelia curled on Rosa's bed, the endless loop of Fidelia's words circling them and holding off, for now, the furry maw of Rosa's hunger, their trip to the dance hall, Rosa pressed against the wall and Fidelia framed by the light, her mouth open to speak. They lay on the bed, wrapped around each other, warm from their circulating breath and still as if sleeping. Mirian and Bernicia—themselves as inseparable as Fidelia and Rosa— who wanted only to be kind and listen too, brought them a single cup of linden tea to share. Fidelia's other sisters stood just outside the room, not brave enough to enter. The tea was weak, the same leaves had been brewed the day before, but the water was hot. Bernicia stumbled on Fidelia's shoe, cast off in the dark and boredom, and reached out for Mirian. Mirian fell forward. The hot water landed on Fidelia and Rosa's bare feet hanging off the bed. The two shouted in unison, swatting at Mirian. Hearing their shouts, Elmo ran towards them, and—not bravely because he didn't think long enough to be brave—scooped up Fidelia's foot and held it against the cool cup of his palm.

"Fidé," he whispered.

Fidelia shrieked in mock modesty and Elmo dropped her foot. Shouting and swatting, the girls drove Mirian, Bernicia, and Elmo out the room and when they were gone turned to each other and laughed, surprising themselves at the sound, then laughed again. There would be time later for bandages and to beg an aloe leaf from Doña Alba, time for the pain to pierce their laughter and shock. But for now, they studied their feet. The water had scalded the top of Rosa's instep and the outside of Fidelia's arch. Their feet must have been overlapping because, when placed together just so, there emerged a detailed map of the splatter, brightly outlined in red: water in the shape of its own fall.

4.

When Fidelia saw Rosa pressed against the damp stucco wall outside the dance hall, no one holding her there but herself, her body straighter than a body could be, what did she see? Did she see what had happened, who had forced their way inside her, what words plugged Rosa's ears? Did she know she was no longer looking at her friend, but at a story that had been told about her, a story in which Rosa's body was only a costume, one that appeared again and again, never relinquished despite its terrible wear? When Fidelia stepped out of the light over the dance hall's back door into the slender corridor that ran between buildings, paths taken by widows selling fruit and children racing to beat the new curfew, did she know that she was stepping out of herself and into that same story? Did she know she left herself in the limen, with not even a place for that self to stand when the door eased shut?

If she had turned and returned to the dance hall, pretending she didn't see Rosa, if she had dragged her friend back inside and found the men and berated them, demanding justice, if she had run past Rosa, into the night and kept running to the sea, even then she could not have stopped her entry into the story. Only if she had stayed still, if she had spun time like sugar and kept them, two paper dolls pinned—one lit in the frame, the other plastered to the wall—could she have stopped what happened next. But she did not have that power and by the time she stood in the doorway, it was already too late. Even before she took Rosa to the dance, even before she herself went to the dance, it was too late for her, the story waiting, feeling no need to rush, waiting to prove that she didn't even have a self in which to step out of. Her body never more than a box of sticks waiting for the story to open and scatter.

Fidelia slipped off her petticoat and tore the bottom strip. With this fabric, she daubed at the blood on Rosa's legs and ankles. She eased Rosa off the wall and tied her own shawl around Rosa's waist. The dress was ruined, but the shawl would cover the tears and stains until they were home. Off the wall, Rosa felt she would tip, that she would shatter on the cobblestones. But Fidelia held her up, moving her hands when Rosa winced—the sound coming from far away—trying to find a point from which she could support Rosa's weight that was not an already-swelling bruise. Away from the dance hall lights, Rosa's face was almost invisible in the shadows, but she smelled of blood, sweat, the butcher's floor, and other smells that were foreign to Fidelia until that night. The smell, Rosa's silence, meant that though Fidelia held her as tightly as she dared, kept Rosa's body as upright as she could, down the back corridors, skirting the Mercado, down Peñitas and Calixto until finally they reached Plaza de la Concordia only a few blocks from their house, she knew she was transporting a foreign form. Her friend's body was burning, and Fidelia feared her own flesh might come off at the contact.

On the outer edge of the plaza, Fidelia's shawl began to slip from Rosa's hips. Fidelia leaned her, still unbending as a yardstick, against a royal palm and, careful not to touch Rosa's skin as much for her own sake as for Rosa's, pulled the shawl back up. Fidelia made a knot and tightened it against her own hand, the shawl itself made of intricate knots her mother had tied years before. Fidelia brought her friend's weight from the coarse bark of the royal palm onto her own body, her arms slick from fear and effort. Across Calle de la Forja and then home.

Doña Alba had seen both girls leave. She had debated trying to stop them. But she reasoned that their punishment for a *committed* crime would be steeper than an *attempted* one. That punishment would have a better chance of leading to them behaving like the good girls families like theirs should be counted on to issue even, and especially, in war time. She waited in her rocker, covered in shadows, for the girls to enter the courtyard. They could not return the way they had left, an improvised path from storm drain to outer balcony that Doña Alba had witnessed only by chance as she emptied her toilet. Instead, they would have to trip right over Doña Alba's toes.

Once inside the courtyard, and thinking it empty, Fidelia leaned Rosa against a pillar. She couldn't carry Rosa up the stairs, and now, in the moonlight through the courtyard, she had to decide whether to awaken someone and who and what to say when she did. Did Rosa need a doctor, is that what she needed, or could it be kept a secret, as these things sometimes were? There were babies born without surnames, and girls who walked unimpeded into the ocean, their white nightgowns floating on the waves. But Rosa's face in the courtyard light was unrecognizable, hardly a face at all, and Fidelia worried that Rosa was still bleeding. She held her friend upright, pressed her shoulders back with the tips of her fingers, and stepped away, just for a moment, to decide. Just a moment without that weight.

But Rosa fell. Fell as she had wanted to. She tipped over the table holding Doña Alba's bougainvillea. The clay pot and soil shattered across the courtyard. Doña Alba stood, and when Fidelia saw her, she screamed as loud as she wished Rosa would, louder than she thought she could, though it took no effort. Fidelia charged the ceiba tree and threw her body against its thorny trunk. It would not yield and neither would she. Doña Alba grabbed her around the waist and pinned her fists under her chin, but she kept screaming. She was still screaming when the courtyard and balconies filled with her and Rosa's family, their parents, their sisters and brothers, ringing the balconies, story after story, and there was no decision to make, no secret left to keep.

5.

At dawn, not having slept, Doña Alba carried her broom to the courtyard to sweep the mess Rosa's fall had made. Instead, she found she wanted to throw the clay pots that covered the courtyard. For them to crash and roll and burst like she was a god playing handball in the clouds. But she had watered the plants the night before, while waiting, and they were heavy, the soil inside rich and damp. Her destruction was slow. The results looked nothing like she felt. She lifted each pot as high as she could and dropped them on the packed hard-as-stone earth. Even cracked, the pots held their shape. One was too heavy to lift more than a few inches off the ground. She pushed the pot over and smacked it with her hand, hoping to send it rolling across the courtyard. The pot hardly bobbled and she felt, in the knuckle of her index finger, a sharp crack. She walked to the cupboard where she kept her tools and, digging with both hands, found the machete.

When she was finished, the courtyard was covered in stalks and leaves and flowers. It smelled of oregano, mint, the insides of calla lily blossoms, all too much green. She hacked at the ceiba tree as well, chopping into its thorns and bark and then arching the machete over her head at any branches she could reach. The fronds fell until she had to wade through the lopped limbs of the plants she had so carefully tended. Their stems and leaves, violently cut, tore at her shins.

In the silence, Doña Alba could hear her own heavy breath and the rustling of vegetation settling. She had been staring at Fidelia for some time before she actually saw her. Fidelia was crouched under the stairwell leading to the second floor. She wore only a slip, her feet bare, hair wet and hanging in strips across her face. Doña Alba focused on the girl, who she had first seen when she was still enclosed in a caul. Fidelia held her face up to Doña Alba, her eyes searching for the old woman's in the dawn light. Doña Alba wanted to spit, but her mouth was dry. Instead, she looked at Fidelia as long as she could and then turned away, as if she hoped she would never see Fidelia again.

When she turned back Fidelia was indeed gone. Elmo had been standing in the shadows behind Fidelia, unnoticed by them both, and when Doña Alba turned, he grabbed Fidelia and dragged her up the stairs. Though Elmo was sweating and frantic, still he was Elmo, Elmo who had loved her all his life. Beneath the stairs, Fidelia had been caught by a terrible thought. Stumbling back to Calle de la Concha, wrapped in her stained shawl, Rosa was silent. The thought came to Fidelia then, in the courtyard, in the silence after Doña Alba stopped her hacking: what if Rosa never spoke again? Though Rosa's words were rare, they were precious. What if Fidelia, the talker, would have no one to interrupt her, no one to prove she wasn't just speaking to herself, no one's voice, but her own. The weight of that silence made her limp. She fell gratefully into Elmo's arms, glad to be lifted, allowing him to swing her back and forth up the steps, through the door to Rafael Agüero's apartment.

Inside, Rosa lay on the sofa, her mother and Bernicia kneeling over her. Elmo dropped Fidelia at his sister's feet and Fidelia was so frightened to see Rosa again—her eyes ruined plums, her lips a smear—that she grabbed for Elmo's hand. He pulled away.

Rafael Agüero stood in a corner—as far from Rosa as he could while still in the same room. His mind was caught in a twist. Before the occupation, in the days when there was someone to tell, he believed such a thing would not have occurred, and would therefore not need to be told. What to do now? He had to make new rules, but he could not make them fast enough. Rafael asked Elmo what he was doing, what his meaning was in treating their Fidé like that, but his mind was caught in the making and the shaping of those new rules and he could not move from the corner.

Elmo didn't hear his father anyway. Elmo began screaming and shouting, he punched walls, scattered furniture, and everyone who heard knew that he was so full of rage and guilt that he must have lost himself, must have put himself aside in the waves of his fury. But no one heard Rosa, no one knows what she said when Elmo laid Fidelia at her feet. Whether she tried to stop him, whether she screamed, whether she turned her head to the wall. When Elmo grabbed Fidelia's shoulders, when he did not call her Fidé or Fidelia, when instead he shook her and said, *You are going to tell us, you are going to tell us what you did*, was Rosa still silent? *Nothing, I did nothing, I didn't say anything. Then why her, why her and not you, you're the same, you made some lie you told them some lie so they went after her instead you betrayed us you slut you.* When Fidelia cried until she couldn't, until Elmo's hands were too tight around her neck, hands that had not touched her since they were children playing in the courtyard, that had kept their distance, save that one time he cupped her burned foot. *No please please no,* until she had no breath to form into words, even such plain, formless words. When Elmo's hands stayed around her neck long past her silence and when his father placed his own hands on Elmo's shoulders, and only then did Elmo let go and Fidelia dropped to the floor. No one knows what Rosa said or did not say. Whether she saw any of this at all.

Rafael carried Fidelia to the courtyard. He cleared a space for her among the branches and broken pottery. Elmo followed him, shaking, his hands over his mouth, until he realized who his hands smelled like and then he did not know where to put them. He wanted to chop them off. Rafael eased him out of the courtyard and back up the steps. He locked Elmo in a room in his apartment that held potatoes and squash and old furniture and steadied himself for the trip to the Armando Castells' door. There was no need. Fidelia's parents stood on their balcony, the empty air of the courtyard hanging between them and Rafael.

The rest of the Agüero Gijóns fled to Rafael's apartment and his older sons barricaded the door from the inside. All day, the moaning and the rosarios from the women of the Armando Castell family could be heard echoing through the courtyard. Rafael stayed crouched in front of the storage room, armed with a broken chair leg and waiting. But the Armando Castells did not charge his door. They did not plunder his sons' apartments, nor—which was what Rafael truly feared on this terrible new day without rules—send in packs of the occupier's police force. It was Diego Armando Castell, Fidelia's father, who asked for the shovel from Doña Alba. At dusk, the Agüero Gijóns heard the peal of metal striking earth. After the sound rang out again, Rafael rose, gathered together his older sons, and joined Diego in the courtyard. When the dirt would not give, Rafael's eldest son thought to make use of the ceiba tree. Together, the men hacked at the roots around the ceiba's base, finally slicing through a large one. Together, they pulled the root out of the earth. From the small cavern the root had made, they gained entry to the ground. They carved with shovels and pry bars until there was a space large enough to hold Fidelia.

6.

Elmo could not forget what his hands had done. He stopped eating. Rosa would not feed him. Rosa's sisters did when they could remember, but Rosa did not. Elmo grew skinnier, skinnier even than Rosa. Soon everyone forgot that Elmo couldn't use his hands, and at dinner Bernicia snuck the meal off his plate bite-by-bite.

One night, their plates empty, he and Rosa sat at

the table alone. He stank from not having changed his shirt in weeks and no one would go nearer to him than they had to. Rosa stared past Elmo in the dark, as if she could see through him, through the closed shutters to the street below. For weeks, there had been whispers that the occupiers were losing interest, that they would move on to a different island, one bigger and richer in sugar and gold. Whispers too that there were rebellions brewing farther west along the coast, or hidden in the jungle, the descendants of the independence fighters gathered and lit smoky fires, announcing their intention to save the island once again. But there had been those whispers and no one believed them. The table was empty save for Elmo's plate and the kerosene lamp that hadn't held kerosene in years. From her seat, Rosa reached out her hands to Elmo's, those lumps of clay, those burning stars. She stretched his hands, one finger at a time, out onto his thighs, smoothing the knuckles and splaying the palms. His hands had become soft as the creases of fat at his neck and knees when he was an infant. Elmo tried to curl his hands back into fists, but Rosa patted them down until they lay flat, spread across his lap, flipped them over for him to see. Rosa stood from the table and Elmo stayed there, staring at the spot where she had sat, the darkness now complete.

Elmo died three days before the liberation, which wouldn't have saved him anyway. Rafael peeled off his clothes, too fetid to keep, to prepare him for the funeral. There was hardly anything left of his son. He resembled more closely a buried stork or dehydrated frog, his skin not like skin, but a film nothing living had coursed through in months. Rafael carried him out of 147 de la Concha so there would be no question of his body leaving the courtyard.

For years, there was talk of adding tile to the dirt floor, but in the end, no one ever did.

Rosa lived in 147 de la Concha for the rest of her long life. Long after the death of her and Fidelia's parents. Long after Fidelia's sisters had left, one moving further inland, Mirian and the others traveling across the ocean, hoping to fold themselves into the stability of that giant continent which hovered its arms, threatening to return and squeeze. Each day, Rosa walked over the courtyard floor, sweeping and sprinkling water, carrying home bread and tomatoes. She cared for Doña Alba as she grew old and sick, and when she died, Rosa became the housekeeper on the bottom floor, cleaning and bustling and knowing everything there was to know about the residents as if she were not an Agüero at all, but an Alba, some long-lost inland cousin come to tend the oregano and take up the sacred duty. If she thought of Fidelia each time she left and entered her home, or never thought of her, or remembered her fiercely for the first few years until her friend began to fade into the dirt, no one knows.

7.

What is known is what is remembered. On the night after the liberation, less than a year after Fidelia was buried, Rosa left 147 de la Concha and walked into the celebrating crowds. No one moved close to her. She seemed to push people away, her body at the center of a small, but impenetrable field. She walked through Plaza de la Concordia, where children sang in the trees, stringing the occupiers' jackets up like streamers, down Peñitas and Calixto, through streets puffed and roaring with free citizens. La

Pieza's famous church, the oldest on the island, was empty, no one lighting candles before the tiny portrait of the Virgin. The whole city was out, every wistful teen and crooked landlord, those who had snitched on the pig's-foot girl and girls like her and those who had not. The people clogged the plaza, old women climbing on park benches, tossing guavas up to the children to keep them singing, mothers threatening to collapse the exterior balconies that had stood empty for so many years. No longer a city turned in on itself, but a city gutted, each vein split and still spilling. But Rosa spoke to no one. She saw few of the faces and she didn't laugh or sing the old anthem or the other banned songs. She didn't look back when the songs became a joyful garble because everyone had forgotten the lyrics, but still wanted to sing. Rosa walked. In Fidelia's whittled heels, Rosa walked down every street she could remember and those she could not. The shoes caught in the cobblestones and turned her ankles until there were no more cobblestones and the heels sunk in the sand and Rosa stood up to her knees in the ocean. The water was lit with firecrackers, shot from the beach to burst above the occupiers' boats as they floated slowly out of the bay. But the horizon seemed closer than it had when there was no hope of rescue or end to the occupation, when she had stood with Fidelia, their dresses tucked between their legs, screaming at the waves and throwing stones as far as they could, as if they could strike the invisible shores on the other side of the world. Rosa turned back from the sea.

I know all this because I saw her, because everyone did, the whole city a witness, and she did not sing the old songs, but she said one name over and over into the pink dawn and the rusted gutters and every corner of the city she knew and did not know. She whispered until her voice was only breath, warming the air, bringing each street back to life, until she became the shape of what she whispered: a dipped brush, slender and full, dyeing the city in the bright pigment of Fidelia's name.

TWO-GALLON HEART

Bound to the earth ten paces from the willow, Frankie calls to her mother. A dream of what she might have been appears solid, white hem dragging through the dust. These moments before dawn are the hardest. The ground will not let go and she must wait. Behind her, houses stretch a hand span of the endless prairie. Houses dropped onto miles of grass without a bird or any sound but rustling mice in the cupboards. Frankie clenches her limbs and doesn't stir. *Come back*, she whispers, *come back*.

Frankie knows the story of her mother and how they found her twelve years ago. She holds the story and follows it. A circle. She is its source.

Come back, she has whispered for years. Today she hears an answer. Today she can feel her mother moving, registers her approach in the tremble of soil. *Vuelvo, hija*, she hears, *Vuelvo*. Today she knows she should not have asked.

The woman who gave birth and some life to Frankie came at the beginning of a storm. Later it was said that she brought the storm. Frankie says she is the storm.

Not a blizzard, when the wind comes up through the plains and casts down blankets until the sleepless know only white, stay inside and forget anything but square houses and bare branches. Then those fade and it is only white before their eyes.

This storm came in summer. The days stretched themselves beneath the sun and the people waded slowly through wet air. In summer, the sky breathes deep and the mind expands beyond the row of houses, the waste of grass. In winter, they would not have believed what they saw.

Nina sits on the porch and waits for Frankie. She knows Frankie is not coming. Nina is the only one who can release her before the ground lets go. This is her task, but today she refuses. They are the same age, but they are not the same. Nina looks up the road and waits. The sounds of the stove heating, eggs cracked, flour stirred.

"Are you finished with your chores?" Jean asks through the screen.

"Yes."

"Where's Frankie?"

Nina is silent. Jean wipes her hands on her apron, brushing off the stiff fibers from the corncobs used to start the fire. Smooths her gray hair with the same long, pale fingers Nina has.

"I told you never to come down without her," Jean says, following Nina's eyes out to the road. "Did she go to the schoolhouse?"

"No," Nina says. "She's out in the fields."

"It's starting to rain. Go get her."

The people stood late into the night watching the storm. On their porches, they watched the dark sky bleached white by lightning. They stood waiting for the next flash, for the world to break in half in front of them. Out of one of these breaks, the woman came.

In this place made of white boards fixed as boxes and a black sliver of dust rarely traced beyond the grove, the people did not know how a woman could appear, as if out of lightning, as if spit from the earth. They did not know how long she had been there. In the storm, they could see only outlines. Dressed in white rags, fine lace torn by layers of root and cloud. A woman, young and full to burst. Her hair was caked in dirt and she was screaming. Tearing at her hair and crawling and getting nowhere, laced to the ground. They stood and watched. They didn't speak. Only one of them had the sense to help her. He climbed down from his wooden railing and ran into the field.

The woman's body was lashed to the dirt. The man stayed with her. He tore his shirt into strips to sop her blood. The others stood on their porches and watched. They knew what to do, had seen it all before, reached into blood—women and horses—and pulled out life. But they didn't move.

"Get up," Nina whispers into Frankie's ear. "Wake up, Frankie. I'm not kidding."

But Frankie can't leave the ground. The roots carry her message and chide her for asking. Nina pulls at her, grabs her arm and rips her nightgown. The rain heavier. Where the water lands, it crackles.

"Frankie, it's time to come home now, please."

Come back, Frankie whispers into the soil. Her bones shake like seeds in a gourd. Frankie's lids and lips are open and moving. She does not see Nina. The thunder bursts and Nina counts. The lightning is coming closer.

"Wake up, Frankie!" Nina shouts, but Frankie does not budge. Nina leaves her on the ground.

The dawn came, the sun baked, the trees sweated in their grove. The storm was a distant memory when the baby finally broke. The woman's blood pooled around her, collected, and was devoured by the earth.

The man and the woman did not say a word. They worked together as if it had been planned, as if everything in their lives had been leading up to blood on the dirt and sweating trees. The people watching were silent too. Only the birds spoke for the child, like humans in their song.

In her bed in Jean's house, the cotton sheets stick to Frankie's skin. She can't peel them off her back. She can't shake this heat. Jean rolls her over, removes the sheets, wipes her with cool rags, drips water into her mouth. Through her fever, Frankie can feel her mother waltzing down the prairie's dirt roads, rapping her fingers against the wet windowpanes. Her mother fogs the glass and shakes the screen door.

Nina sits by her with a book open on her knees. Frankie's whispers turn to shouts. Air scrambling its dirty nails up cracked pipes and tongue crashing into teeth.

"Quiet," Nina says. "You'll wear yourself out."

"You've quit reading," Frankie says. "What are you looking at?"

"Nothing," Nina says. She presses her pages and crosses her ankles. "Just the clouds."

"My foot the clouds. My stinky, sweaty foot."

The pages of Nina's book turn slowly, her silent refusal.

"We're going to have a visitor," Frankie whispers. "She's coming soon."

"No one's coming, Frankie. No one ever comes here. Just be quiet."

"Oh, yes, she is," Frankie says. "She's coming soon. Better watch out."

A robin slams into the window and Nina runs out the door.

"Open the window and let him in," Frankie calls after her. She is sweating again. Holding the bed frame, she pulls herself up and out, blood rushing, head throbbing around a new grown beast. She opens the window. The wind off the prairie dries her skin. The robin watches its reflection melt into a girl with wild hair.

"Come in," Frankie says. Out the window a sea of grass that was once sea. She leaves the window open and climbs back into bed. "Come in."

The woman was not known in the town and she was strange. They saw her only as they could, as the colors of the storm she came in, because they could imagine no elsewhere. Midnight blue as the space between stars, stark white as the lightning that makes them. She was revolving to them, a twist so far toward one edge she was expelled, transformed onto the other. They could not imagine her birth, on an island where gods swam in rivers and rode people like horses, where she had prayed at the base of a ceiba tree. They could not imagine the paths that brought her to their door. They who knew only the white houses, the black road, who called those the colors of night, ignoring all indications of creation.

They did not have the words for her and so could not see her. Frankie, Frankie they could see.

"How did they get in here?" Nina says.

"Through the window," Frankie says.

"But how?"

"I called them."

Nina and Frankie crouch on the bed, close together, knees tucked and looking up. Birds circle the room, dropping feathers, landing on shelves, pecking idly at the quilt. Wrens nestle in the bureau, thrushes dancing between the curtains. They fill the air, fluttering out of reach, never colliding.

"Who's coming, Frankie?" Nina says.

Frankie rocks slowly, wearing a furrow into the mattress. "No one you know."

"Who, then?"

"My mother."

Nina stays silent. She doesn't like this ghost woman and her tale. It has been years since Frankie spoke of her mother, since Frankie last believed she would come. Since Nina carried bruises from Frankie's fists when she didn't.

"But the birds?" Nina asks. Feathers cover the bed.

"I called them," Frankie says. A blue-black feather falls and settles on her shoulder.

She never flinches, Nina thinks. There are hundreds of birds in their room and they will be gone in the morning. She could slap Frankie and Frankie would hardly notice.

With dawn the man's wife stirred from her trance, realized new human flesh shivered within her reach. Crossed to the grove and wrapped the child. It seemed well, the baby, and the woman too, though she left the next day. Swallowed once more by gaping prairie. But her husband faded. As if it was his blood that spilled on the ground, his blood that the earth drank without pause. They found him the next morning beneath the willow. He had climbed out of bed at night and fallen there. Birds circled above.

Frankie's mother is sitting at the kitchen table. In the wicker seat that Frankie helped mend last fall, in the too-stark light of a morning without clouds. The day will be hot. But the woman is not sitting. The wicker does not bend beneath her, such substances cannot notice her weight and though Jean serves her coffee, speaks to her of the changing price of small things, she can't really see her either. Only Frankie can see her dark hair bleached red at the tips by sun and woven with reeds. Limbs like willow branches, lithe and pulled back, ready to snap. Only Frankie can see that beneath her brown skin her mother glows green, like trillium at night. Frankie sees past the women's words about the weather and the road, sees straight to her mother's rapidly beating bird-heart. Jean sets down toast, raspberry jam, and a blue-speckled creamer. She agrees to the heavy weight of dust on a woman's feet. But only Frankie knows what the apparition means.

¿Vienes conmigo? the woman silently asks, the words thrumming on the dust motes between her and Frankie. *Are you coming with me?*

Frankie doesn't answer.

This morning should have been brown bread and yellow butter, red jam running down wrists, orange yolk spilling across the blue forget-me-not patterned plates. Frankie and Nina's legs swinging barefoot and tomcats weaving between their ankles like reams of silk. Instead, the morning is broken. Jean's hands shake as she folds the cornbread batter, heats up more coffee, darts her eyes between Frankie and this, what? This woman not-quite-a-mother and not-quite-a-stranger. Four cups in a quart, four quarts in a gallon and Jean's is a two-gallon heart. That is all it can hold and it should not be asked to hold more.

Without the strange woman at the table, Jean can look across the kitchen and see Frankie. Her too-long limbs, her too-quick tongue, her too-solid body and light-brown skin that anyone could read whatever history they wanted on. But with this woman seated on her wicker chair, accepting coffee, Jean looks at Frankie and sees only her husband when the woman first came—sees only death.

They eat in silence, Nina and Frankie staring at the woman, their tongues held on a tight leash by Jean's shaking hands. Nina goes to the porch to look for the woman's bags or a trunk to spy into, but the porch is empty. Frankie slips into the cupboard beneath the sink and waits to be looked for. Her absence goes unnoticed. Jean and her mother talk in careful, guarded voices, arms crossed. Talking about Frankie and they do not notice that Frankie is not talking too. Why should she be? Frankie starts rustling, then banging. Jean pulls her out of the cupboard and exiles her for eavesdropping, but she slips back, the women's words barely audible over her own rushing blood.

Nina eases her fingers, cool and never damp, around Frankie's wrist and the rushing slows.

"Where did your mother come from?" Nina says.

Frankie stays silent so she doesn't have to say she doesn't know.

"Will you call the birds for her?" Nina says.

"No, I won't do anything for her."

"You won't leave me, either?"

"No."

In the storm, between her screams, the woman whispered to the man that her name was Armando Castell, but if he heard her words, he died before he could repeat them. She gave no first name and said the words unwillingly, as if she spoke not to be remembered, but because a power beyond her compelled her speech. The only soul left that had even touched the child was the man's wife. And what could she do? She could not hold her once, but she was bound to her. She could not look at her once, but thirst to see her. That was the only way the child survived; the spell she cast at birth. Jean gave her food, called her Frances. Put her down in the crib beside her granddaughter whose parents were lost to last year's fever. And never locked the door at night so the child could leave the house and fall where she was called—the dirt beneath the willow.

"Frankie, why don't you show her where she can sleep?" Jean says.

On the porch, moths batter against the screen door. Jean does not know what word to call Frankie's mother. It should have been settled long ago, but by the time she realized her lapse it was too late.

"I sleep outside," the woman says and turns to Frankie. "Don't you?"

"Of course not," Jean speaks before Frankie can, as if to erase her knowledge of the willow and dirt.

Frankie slips between the railing of the porch and swings underneath. Crouched beneath the floorboards, in the dirt of swallows' roosts, she nurses those first words: *Don't you. Don't you.* The first words ever spoken to her by her mother, unless she counts the calls from the soil before daybreak and the branches rapping a secret language on frosted window-panes. Frankie does not need to count those words anymore. *She came waltzing down that road for me.*

And Frankie is burning to show her. That she is not soft for her goose feather pillow, that she too can speak and call. She leaps onto the porch. She lifts her arms and closes her eyes. She stamps her feet with all her strength, bending the floorboards, lodging splinters into her toes, kicking up the dust Jean patiently swept away. *Come, come to me.*

Nina looks up to the horizon, sure she sees a flock brewing there. She looks to the faces of Jean and the woman and she is proud for the first time that she knows Frankie, proud to have shared her secrets all those years.

But there is no sound except for heat lightning. Even the trees are silent. Frankie opens her eyes and the faces once fixed on hers have turned away. She doesn't dare seek Nina's, who remembers Frankie's promise not to call the birds for her mother and picks at the dirt packed under her big-toenail.

"That's just something Frankie does," Jean says. "A play-game when she's nervous."

"Aren't you a little old for play-games, hija?" the woman asks.

Her words recreate the world. The birds are remembered as that, no more real than the sound of the ocean in a cupped hand. A whole existence crumbles and a new one is born. In this world, there are only the lines of the chair and the porch, nothing hidden in the grass, no voices in the soil. For Nina this world is bleak, but Frankie has been waiting and she enters silently.

"I came for you," the woman says. "Are you coming with me?"

Frankie can only nod.

"It will be hard for you," the woman says. "I have no home like this. The air is cold and the ground is wet. I walked out of this sea of grass and gave you life. If you come with me, I will tell you your name."

The woman hadn't asked for a child, started in some nameless town with a face never remembered. The new weight got in her way. It tried to fix her to a single roof, to a roof at all. She had no songs to sing, no lulling to calm the approach of night. But she had not meant to leave her child behind. She merely continued moving and did not realize the weight was gone until her footsteps back to it had blown away. *I am not a mother*, she had said, and her dreams drained back to silence.

"Frances already has a name," Jean says. "But you're right. It would be too hard a life. She's safer here."

Frankie knows any words would betray her heart. She has to appear solid as the once-speaking earth. *I called her back*. Fingernails pierce half-moons into her palms. *She came back for me.*

"Yes, a hard life," echoes the woman. "Too hard for her."

"No," Frankie says. She can't control herself. "It's not too hard."

The woman rises from her chair, steps across the porch, and strikes Frankie. Her cheek swells and blooms red.

"You don't tell me what to do," the woman says.

Her thumb slides down Frankie's hot cheek and drops to her lip like a petal over water. She can make the seconds stretch. By the time she turns her back on Frankie and sits down in the rocker, Jean knows there is nothing on earth that would let her give Frankie to this woman. Frankie knows there is no force to stop her from going.

"You should leave in the morning," Jean says to the woman. "You should leave and not come back."

Frankie hears this, but she knows she can't stay within Jean's walls. She asked the ground for her mother and her mother came. She cannot deny her source.

Frankie and Nina climb into bed, both knowing they do so for the last time. Frankie kicks off the quilt. Nina reaches down and folds it evenly at the base of the bed. Under the sheets they are still, Frankie hot and Nina cool. The air between them is damp with the coming storm, but they keep their heads covered.

"Will you go?" Nina says.

"Yes."

"Will you go without me?"

"Yes."

Nina falls asleep and Frankie stares through the white sheet, lit with moonlight and grazing her eyelashes. Rising and falling with her breath, the sheets mimic the motions of the clouds, but there is no pull to the earth tonight. The roots are silent and she can hear only the drumbeat of her own heart. Frankie leaves the bed, leaves Nina, and wanders the house. Each piece of furniture carries its own scent, held in for years and exhaled that night. On the rocker, Frankie smells Nina's fear when Jean was bit by a rattlesnake last summer. Rubbing the corners of the kitchen table releases the musk of a baby screech owl she weaned years ago, whose claws dug into the wood. She smells winter and Nina's waiting feeling.

Frankie walks out the door, catches her mother's scent on the newborn wind, knows she is still close. She crawls under the porch to wait. The moon lights up sparks of dust. The sparks rise between the porch floorboards. Frankie holds her breath, begging for a call, but tonight the earth is silent.

Nina is not asleep. How could she be with a sound, so close to thunder, rushing through her? She feels Frankie leave the bed, moves her hand into the warm impression where her body was. She closes her eyes again and when she opens them, she is pinned to the ground beneath the willow. Her face and limbs locked to the dirt.

A breeze stirs up the dirt below the porch and brings with it a change. Frankie's mother is moving. She makes no sound when she leaves, but Frankie smells the soft skin behind her ears, the heat underneath her hair. Frankie rises from beneath the porch. She follows that scent and she does not look back.

Had the wind changed, had Frankie chosen to turn for a last glance on the house that once held her life, she would have seen Nina. Just a faint outline of white cloth against a black sky. When the earth inhaled, it let go of Nina and she ran, with no scent or sight to follow, just the electric braid tying her to Frankie. She couldn't see Frankie, but she kept running, following that braid. Soon Nina tired, she stumbled, but she kept moving.

All night long, the wind did not change and Frankie did not look back. The three walked: the woman, Frankie, and Nina, away from the house, away from Jean, down the dirt road, each unheeding what was behind them, caught unwillingly in the same orbit, all hurtling forward.

PALM CHESS

La Habana, Cuba, May 29, 1943
On the short, bumpy flight from Miami to Havana, I sat be-
side a Galician widow and whispered to her as she slept. In my
awkward Spanish, I hissed that I am a filmmaker, savoring the
words finally spoken aloud. "No sound, black and white film,
my preference." On the tray table, my prayer card of la Virgen
de la Pieza sat balanced against my cigarette case, the Virgin's
face creased, the card's corners rounded. The widow slept, mouth
open, dentures slipping back. I eased her fan from her lap and
practiced opening and closing it with only a flick of the wrist.
"I'll be filming alone, deep in the campo," I continued. "Miles
from where any tourist goes." I didn't mention Claude, but I
repeated I and alone enough that he might as well have stood
over us in the aisle, clinking his brandy, winking at the stew-
ardesses in their matching skirt-suits and banana-printed cra-
vats, his hand gripping the back of my seat. After my cigarette
case was empty, I sucked on the end of my braid. I promised
Claude, I'd never cut it. After my second drink, I sniffed the
prayer card, but it had long lost any identifying scent.
The widow woke just before we landed, on the sharp
descent between ocean clouds. When I wouldn't let go of her
fan, she cupped my hands in hers, thumbing the bare base of
my ring finger, smooth from the two years when it carried a
wedding ring. Perhaps she could sense Claude as well, because

she looked behind us and though her smile remained, it contorted in on itself, like she was tolerating a nasty smell. She took the fan from my fingers, opened it effortlessly, and lay it down on her lap. The painted lace depicted a formal tea scene, invisible when folded, of two women serving cakes. Behind them, a giant dog floated. The widow's hands were covered in rings, large and gaudy, some paste, but her wedding ring was real, a small, opaque ruby circled by diamonds, the gold band thin as a nail clipping. She removed the ring and slipped it onto my finger.

"I'm a filmmaker," I repeated, to hear the words again, to see if she had been listening, faking sleep. But she was silent. Her ring caught on my knuckle, she spit and rubbed until she'd pushed the band to the base of my finger. If she had spoken, I would have resisted her gift, not out of any moral reason, but because I didn't want it. Her silence acknowledged the selfishness of her act. With the ring, I fear Claude is somehow more likely to catch me.

PALM CHESS:

CAMERA OPENS ON:
A woman's face (Angela's, if she'll let me film her), her eyes open. It is unclear whether she is lying on the ground or standing. Her long braid unraveled, her hair frames her face like she has fallen into a hard, dark pillow. Slight tension in the neck, chin flung back. From this angle she might even be headless, blinking out her final moments.

CUT TO:
Church alcove, incense smoke rises. Votive candles flicker as if a door has opened behind them.

CUT TO:
A man's legs, slowly walking down the center aisle. The shadow of his legs on the pews.

CUT TO:
The woman's face. Her eyes closed. She is sleeping on the dark stones of the church floor. White dress, satin, plastered to her, greasy ruffles around sleeves and hem. She is barefoot, black hair loose, makeup smeared, not virginal. Strings of beads around her neck and wrists.

CUT TO:
Man's shadow, in profile, on confession grate. He walks with a hand outstretched. Man's shadow over woman's body. Man kneels. Votive candles gut out.

La Habana, June 4, 1943
In terms of the script, the man chases her out of the church and into the bright light. She takes gulps of air, as if she had been underwater. The man stalks her. The shot is played in reverse and slow motion—dream time, agonizingly slow, the movement of her hair and dress does not match her body's gestures. She is back in the church by the end of the film, but I want it to feel like ages have passed, all the possible footsteps and rump sashays, back before pleated skirts and churches, legs framed by white ginger flowers, feet treading the same ground as rodents, frogs, nesting birds. She'll return to the church, but I want the scenes to linger and build so that when she finally opens the door again, we feel like she's been reborn.

I know there are certain scenes I need. The scene in the jungle, the night market, the church. If Angela refuses, I can set up a tripod. I can pay men to walk towards and away from me. I can kill a chicken and smear my hands with its blood. I can carry my own camera. But there are specific angles I don't know how I'll catch.

And I don't know if he catches her? His shadow falls on her, but does he?

La Habana, June 7, 1943

This city glitters with film stars and little moons trying to lock an orbit. They all know Claude. They've heard of me, they say, squinting a little and trying to guess which woman I am, the former wife or the current lover, but even of those choices there are long columns of names to pick from. I slide past them, off the dance floor, out of the glitzy city center, and I buy a train ticket to bring me over the mountains to La Pieza. The once-prosperous city has been mostly destroyed by mold, hurricanes, the wars of independence, the American occupations, but the oldest church on the island still stands and the miniature of the Virgin remains in her alcove, her eyes flat and dark. La Pieza's Virgin is only as big as the palm of your hand yet she once had a purpose, the last stop on a centuries-old pilgrimage. In La Pieza, they say that La Caridad del Cobre, should really be La Caridad de la Pieza, that the Virgen appeared there, over their water, pregnant, to save their three boys, that for centuries she would disappear from her church in Cobre and appear in La Pieza, her true home.

Angela has gone ahead of me—she's studying the island's dance traditions, making field recordings. Good research for the role I hope she'll take. She says she'll bring me to some of the more public religious performances and perhaps, in time, to others.

I don't want Claude to know I have arrived on the island. I hope he thinks I am still in Miami, still debating whether to leave without him. I want him to believe my silence as petty, female. I used to be silent for days. Awake in bed and him asleep. Gnashing the pillow, gobbling up comforters. Once, after we'd married, I disappeared for a week—used up all my welcomes sleeping on friends' Murphy beds—and when I returned, he made no mention of my absence. As if I'd been out on an afternoon errand and he'd been able to get a good bit of writing done. Soon he'll learn where I'm headed, but I want to get there first.

Dust, palms, sea snaking by the train window,
June 8, 1943
I want a woman watching the film to enter and be swallowed. I want the film to have a specific purpose and function, a specific shape to fit a specific vacancy. You see the swaying palms, you watch the woman watch the men, and then the palms sway on the inside of your skull, projected there, you are the woman clenching her beads, you see her and know to be her. Lost inside her, you forget her and yourself and you move in this new world.

So far, the script is just notes. I write the scenes when I can catch them, but sometimes writing is like stripping skin and spinning it through a needle. It clogs, it hurts.

La Pieza, finally, June 9, 1943
I arrived in the dusty town—now just a widening in the road before it meets the ocean, a few crumbling colonial buildings flanked by thick jungle and rattling sugarcane—and Angela showed me to the little room she'd found, overlooking the sea wall. A green rectangle with an iron bed, green lizards and an iron balcony, ceilings receding out of reach, catching exhaled heat. An old man brings us café con leche and white bread flaky with lard.

Angela, raised between Miami, Tampa, and La Habana, with her dark hair wrapped in a bright scarf, her easy Spanish, looks and sounds like she belongs here. We drink warm rum in her room with the shutters closed. The acrid smell of green coffee beans on a roasting pan slinks up the stairs. She points to the ring the old Galician woman gave me and raises her eyebrows.

"*I thought you left him.*"

"*It's not mine," I say. "But I can't get it off.*"

She turns up the volume on the field recordings. She won't let me speak of Claude.

"*Will you take the role?" I ask her. "Will you play the woman?*"

Her silence the most solid answer. I need her, you see, and she knows it. But long ago I promised not to write about her, not to film her. I promised and I broke that promise. Many times, she reminds me.

We talk instead about the men she's met here, who all propose marriage. When I rise to leave, she says, "I hope you didn't come here looking for a shoulder to cry on and a warm body to hold. You're dear to me, but I'm not doing that again. I have my own things to carry."

I nod.

"*I got you this room," she says. "But I didn't come here for you. It's my home too.*"

La Pieza, June 10

My equipment is impossible. It is less the weight of my Bolex, my arms have grown used to holding her above me or at my hips, but everything else. The tripod, the case, the lenses and their hatred of the unavoidable humidity, the reels of film and their tendency to unravel and twist.

I spent everything from Claude's last two checks on my Bolex. She is a marvel. I've practiced holding her steady, practiced the slight movements to change an angle, to alter a mood. When I can shoot with nothing else but her on my shoulder, I am more agreeable. I fade into her clicks and whirs, my lids suturing to the damp eyecup, my mascara smearing on the view-finder. But usually more is needed.

Angela takes me to the sugarcane fields and the streams where women wash clothes. I film the women walking down the dirt road through the palms, the sea wall behind them. They wear bright scarves on their heads and balance woven baskets on top of the scarves. Bananas, wood, dried corn. Some are dressed in all white—the newly initiated. I know what the colors of the beads they wear mean—allegiance with a partic-ular godhead—but little beyond that. When I try to film the beads, the wrist twists, the shirt sleeve slips, the hand moves to brush me away.

Angela can get past the blank stares and silences, but I speak and cannot reach them. There is something hurried about me, something wasteful in my energy to capture this and that. It smacks of the country I was raised in and cannot shake.

La Pieza, June 11

At night I go over that idiotic fight with Claude at Marlo's be-fore I left Chicago. It was about the artists he and Marlo are newly enamored with. "The Primitives," Marlo calls them, "The Innocents." All their work is the same and all their stories are the same, though they purport to be different people and one of them is even a woman. Their eyes are big and blue and sad or big and blue and joyful, either way always blue and always about to brim over. They say they know nothing about art, though each of them attended an academy in New York or, worse, the Continent. Marlo brought out their paintings for us to admire—two-dimensional imitations of West African masks, landscapes copying Aboriginal paintings.

I waved my wine glass dangerously close to the paintings and told Marlo what I thought of them. "You cannot pretend to be innocent," I said. "They're thieves and they know it!"

"Carmen Castell de Armando," Claude said, (trying and failing to use my full name—he always mixed up the order or forgot a name or two). *"We all steal. Even you."*

I turned from him and spat on the nearest painting. Claude grabbed me, he told me I'd gone mad, and I pretended it was the art that I hated, that made me writhe against him. He twisted me and I howled and bit. Together with Marlo, he carried me out of the apartment and dropped me on the sidewalk.

Two of the Innocents stood there, waiting to be let into Marlo's salon. They were languorously frightened, clutching each other's skinny waists, eyes soggy as expected.

"Don't worry," I hissed. "Your precious thefts remain unharmed above."

Marlo leaned out of the balcony window. "I won't throw down the key until you've calmed yourself," he said.

"We're hungry," the Innocents cried.

"I'm off," I shouted. "I'm already gone."

La Pieza, June 15
Angela will bring me to a dance tonight. A celebration in honor of Shangó. I must be silent and I cannot bring my camera. But that is why I am here, I tell her, to bring my camera.

"Not yet," Angela says. "You must wait until you are trusted."

She comes to my room at dusk, with two other women, both much older than us and dressed in bright red dresses. I am not to have eaten and I must carry gifts, offerings both for the people dancing and the gods they dance for. The women check my pockets, as if I could hide my camera there. I gesture to my Bolex, locked away in its heavy black case under the bed. You would know if I carried it, I want to say. With her on my shoulder, I am unmistakable.

We walk through the town until the scent of the fish market is interrupted by the scent of green and smoke. We approach a house almost buried in grasses. The women tell me to close my eyes.

La Pieza, June 16

While some talk of the Virgen appearing in these hills, others say that if you ask in the right way, if you carry the right gifts, you will receive God. Bearing down on your body, convulsing and riding you. You are no longer self, but horse for gods to gallop into the jungle, dig at the roots of the palms until your fingers bleed, dance and then run to the sea. God might drown you, there is that chance, but more likely she will let you keep dancing. The gods prefer devotion to the suffering they are capable of bringing on the body. When the gods press into your skin, they silence you, they empty you of yourself, push you out through your fingertips and there, at the distance between skin and air, you disappear. It must be such a gift to jump out of one's skin. Not a haunting, but a transformation to salt on the wind, spread over a crowd of outstretched tongues.

La Pieza, June 17

What I didn't tell the Galician widow on the plane:

1. *That, though my mother was from the island, I've never been.*
2. *That, like a woman in a tale, my mother was once a priestess, and, also like a woman in a tale, she was revered in her old land and ignored in her new one.*
3. *That none of the scenes I've written for my film are actual rituals. I imagine stages, what I think I'll see. The scenes are flat because of this, empty. I feel I should know them. But why? My mother left her altars behind when she crossed the sea, married, refused to speak of who she was or had been. I close my eyes and try to hear her singing, conjure the sound of beads clinking on her wrists,*

*her voice wrapped in cigar smoke, but I hear only what
I think I've lost. I'm trying to remember, but it's something that's not mine.*

*4. That I asked my mother nothing when she was alive.
Nothing of any importance.*

CAMERA OPENS ON:

Two old women washing clothes in a stream. Their heads
are covered and their feet bare. They dip the clothes in the
stream and then lash them against the stones beside their
feet. One woman smiles up at the camera.

CUT TO:

The woman from the opening shot stands near them. An old
woman smiles and beckons her closer. The woman reaches
towards the pile of wrung-clean clothes on the rock. The
older women shake their heads, one crooks her finger and
beckons the woman towards the water.

CUT TO:

The old women stand on the shore, edging the younger
woman into the water. She looks behind her and sees that
the opposite shore is far away. The current is fast. The two
old women hold out their hands, smiling. They step towards
her, as if nudging a child gently into bed.

June 19

*I fear Claude is getting closer. I think I smelled him last night
at the night market, in between the plantain stalls. I buried my
face in watercress to shake his stink, but it remains. He must
have discovered my ticket stubs, or asked Moné or Marlo where
I was going. He's not here yet, maybe one town over, maybe still
in La Habana, whoring it up.*

Claude, perhaps I did not make myself clear. I am making the film alone. You are not invited. It was not your name on the grant. It was mine. It is not you who is writing the script, it is me. Carmen Fidelia Beracierto Armando Castell. I am the one whose history is buried in ground I know nothing about. You are not her.

The night before I left him—though he did not know there was any extra importance to my stance, my pert lips, my clean fingernails—I told him about a dream I had. I dreamt of a glowing, white figure walking through the whole world, starting on the streets, at market stalls, in narrow shops. Then he enters a home and another, each from a different land—India, Bangkok, trailing his fingers round the insides of a wood-slat tent, folding back the hide door of a yurt, pushing into Buddhist monasteries and Shinto shrines. Grabbing what he wants: one thing here, one thing there, wrapping himself in tapestries, slinging a Yoruba mask over his shoulder, joyful, elated, the world at his fingertips, the world an oyster, he a knife, silver and pry. He empties the object of all meaning. He leaves dust in his wake.

I know it's Claude I smell. His body leaking into the sea air, letting me know he's landed.

CAMERA OPENS ON:
The woman walking through the market. Neat piles of bananas and mangoes, malanga and yuca that smell of dirt. People move behind and around the stalls, a daily ritual, conferring and debating. It is earlier than the church scene—a few days or lifetimes before. She wears a tight black dress, sweats in the heat. No shoes. The camera is positioned at the opposite end of the market. At first, she is just one of the crowd, but she sees the camera and walks towards us in indolent steps. She moves closer, closer, and then she walks

past. The camera turns with her. Only then do we see that she was not following the camera, but two men, sugarcane workers, carrying their machetes and walking back towards the edge of town. She follows them down a long dirt road, with high grasses on either side. She runs a few steps to keep up with the men, but never gets too close. If they see her, they do not stop or look back. They turn off the road and into the dense brush.

CAMERA CUTS TO:
Late afternoon, the men have returned to town. The shadows lengthen in front of the three figures. The woman's shadow comes close to grazing the men's heels, but never quite manages contact. The men do not look back at her.

CUT TO:
The torchlights of the night market. The men's faces are clear beneath the lamps of the stalls they stop at, light bouncing off their cheekbones and foreheads. They bend over cages of pigeons and whisper to the birds. The woman stops behind a stall selling lentils and chickpeas in burlap bags.

CUT TO:
The men walk out of the market and into the dark street. Just before they leave the torchlight, they turn to the woman. They know she has been following them. They make no reply to her question, her incessant footsteps, legs swishing after them. They answer neither yes nor no.

La Pieza, June 20
Expectant mothers, grieving mothers, all mothers used to walk barefoot to see La Pieza's Virgin. Like them, she is pregnant, waiting for a prayer. They would walk down the dirt roads,

through the swamps, over river stones and rough gravel, the mosquitoes landing on their skin. The longer they walked to get to her, the louder their prayer. The Virgin was a window. They pressed their faces to the open air.

My mother was from La Pieza and she carried this worn prayer card of la Virgen de la Pieza in her purse, even after she had given up all the other idols. I didn't know she carried it until she was already gone. For a few months the card smelled like her.

I try to retrace the steps to the ritual from the other night. Angela says I am not to do this, but if I can film a bit of the cold fire, the footprints in the dirt, then I won't have lost so much time. Angela shouldn't have worried, I traced the perimeter of the town several times, but I cannot find the trail the women led us down.

CAMERA OPENS ON:

A muddy river, men and women in white wade into the water, it stains their clothes. The camera is positioned above as if on a bridge, a spy. The people plunge into the water, and sink deep, first their torsos, then shoulders, finally their white headdresses disappear into the rushing current.

La Pieza, June 27

Angela says if I want to film the rituals I cannot do so as an outsider or a guest. The rituals are private, she says, and a secret.

"That is the problem," I say. "I want to film them because they are a secret."

"But some are more secret than others. Some can never be captured and taken away, some, however, could be."

"Take me to those then."

"They won't let me," Angela says. "They are less secret, but even so too secret for an outsider, an uninitiated. One who had

been seated however, she would not be practicing theft to film them, she would be guided by God and could not commit evil. She would be a part of the ritual and therefore she would remove nothing, she would merely be carrying the ritual with her."

"How long would that take?"

"Months," Angela says. "A year. But you must mean it for life. Otherwise, it is theft."

I do not argue, of course, she is right.

"Theft," she continues, "is only permissible under certain circumstances. It must be intimate. It must hurt you too."

But Claude is coming closer. I do not have months or a year.

La Pieza, June 29

I return to the church. The Virgen de La Pieza is unimpressive, as everything you've worked hard to reach. My fingertips hovering just above the canvas, I trace the Virgen's lips, her outstretched palms, I move my hands slowly around the sooty frame. I want to hook my nails under the painting, into the crumbling stone. To pry the painting out of the wall in one sure jerk. It would fit in the palm of my hand, and I am hungry for it, the way looking at an infant's chubby knees makes you gnash your teeth. The church is empty. But it would cost me nothing to steal this painting. I am the one who needs to pay. The reel can be looped, Claude. How do you steal yourself?

CAMERA OPENS ON:

The woman's face on the wet sand. A wave washes over her face and shoulders. She arches her neck in pleasure.

CUT TO:

Wider shot: the waves over her body, she turns slowly in the sand. Her hair is soaked, braid wrapped around her neck like wire.

CUT TO:
The man runs his fingers down the woman's spine. He cups her feet in his hand.

CUT TO:
The woman's face below water. She opens her eyes.

La Pieza, July 3

Claude's scent burrows into me, but I want to coat myself in my own stink instead. I want to be possessed by myself alone. I close the windows during the day and I let the room bake, even the green lizards flee and the June bugs emerge, believing it's night. When I open the windows, it feels like I am swimming. I buy more mangoes than I can carry and pay the boy with the pigeons to help, but on the way home I see a stand of bananas, each fruit only as long as your thumb. I give some to Angela, but I keep too many. I eat with my hands. I tear off the skin of the mangoes and the flesh swells under my fingernails, stringy and orange. I eat and eat. I eat so many bananas that I make myself sick and Luis, who brings the café, pounds on the door of the latrine, first in anger, then sympathy. But in the morning, I'm still hungry. I want my skin as soft as the bananas' skin, my eyes as soft. I am waiting to smell only like them.

Claude, are you on that one dirt road that leads to this town?

CUT TO:
The woman kneels on a jungle path, knees in the spongy dirt, hands clasped in prayer. Between her hands appears a sugarcane knife. She grips the knife and reaches for her neck. She saws at her braid, the knife catching and stuttering until finally she has cut straight through.

CUT TO:

The woman's open palms: her thick braid stretched across them, still as a sleeping snake.

La Pieza, July 5

My room is empty. I can no longer bear the heat. I walk across the hall to Angela's. She is playing one of her field recordings and dancing to it. She adds a pirouette and a jeté to the intricate footwork she has learned here. On her table is a telegram to me from Claude. I read it quickly, but I already know what it says—it was sent from La Habana.

Angela is not silent to teach me a lesson about Claude, she is speaking only to herself. She forgets I'm there. The shutters are closed, but a thin stripe of yellow light bisects the room. She dances in and out of the light, her feet kick up dust.

She is crying. She sees me and stops dancing. She stops the field recording. She stands in profile in the light, her tears bright. She starts dancing again. She is still crying and for reasons she won't be sharing. I get the Bolex and film her. I move close, to catch the shimmering drops of tears on her cheeks and sweat on the brim of her upper lip. The shadow made by her chin over her collarbone, the shadow on her face of her arm rising slowly into the air. Her body is speaking and not to me.

Angela takes the Bolex from my shoulder. She spins the camera on me. With one hand, she balances the camera in the crook between her neck and shoulder. With the other, she threads her fingers through my shorn hair. Though my braid is gone, my hair rough and springy where I cut it, her touch seems to take hours. She takes what she wants. I know the lighting is perfect.

FINAL SCENE:

OPEN ON:

Dense forest growth. The woman emerges from the leaves, pushes aside giant, wet blossoms. The water stains her skirt, drips from her chin. The ground beneath her is unstable, holding millennia of secret, animal pathways.

CUT TO:
The woman breaks through a layer of leaves to a clearing. Soft grasses beneath her feet. We see her fully for the first time. Around her neck, she wears the thick braid of her own hair.

CUT TO:
A collapsing house, several stories tall, with a courtyard in its center, surrounded by the jungle. A ceiba tree grows out of the courtyard: its buttress roots spread over the open ground, its branches reaching through the bare roof beams, up into the sky. But the front door of the house is freshly painted, and crisp swaths of bright fabric hang from the windows. Smoke billows from the courtyard and out the door.

CUT TO:
The woman on the porch, between the narrow columns and intricate shutters. She looks into the camera. Jasmine vines cast shadows on her face. She brings her hand to the half-open door. Hung from a nail on the door sway strings of red seed beads, cowrie shells, a wreath of herbs. She unwraps the braid from her neck and balances it on the nail, weaves the beads into and around her hair. She pushes the door open and steps inside the house.

FINAL SHOT:
The door ajar, the woman gone. Instead of shadows or an empty, collapsed room, the door opens to the sea. The waves crash slowly on the shore.

THE NIGHT OF THE ALMIQUI

Monday

It was just before the revolution began in earnest. The secret police still roamed the capital's humid streets without fear, torturing and disappearing who they wished. The guerrillas' victories had been paltry—a few granaries, an unguarded armory. The particular rebel band that would eventually ride to the capital on stolen tanks through cheering crowds was still exaggerating how many troops they had to American reporters, troops that were still mostly intellectuals from wealthy families with no knowledge of the terrain they sought to conquer, who didn't know to hide their leather boots at night from the giant land crabs that roamed the mangroves, didn't know how hungry they would get, how long they could stay hungry, how long it took for the body to eat itself. Yet they were learning. The peasants taught them how to eat very little and the hunters taught them how to move silently and women snuck messages in their girdles and organized burro trains that brought rice and cornmeal and ammunitions. The island kept them alive, week after week, month after month, as they all waited.

The ceiba trees did not notice. The land crabs and the nightjars and the almiqui, a nocturnal rodent considered extinct for a hundred years, did not notice. But for those praying for the rebel's victory, a change began. Something had shifted in the island's very language. The word for each animal and plant morphed. Quotidian items became ghostly and unrecognizable, as if they had cast off their old names and wore only a name of waiting. For surely the revolution, when it came, would rewrite the whole island anew.

Even in Campo Chico, backwater to the east bordered by jungle and cane, people noticed this change. La Abuela, five months pregnant and decades younger than her name suggested, crept downstairs to open the small sewing shop below her rooms. She'd worked at the shop for years, first sleeping under the counter when El Papi threw her and Benny out of his mansion and later moving to the rooms above when the owner grew too old to climb the stairs, though she kept firm hold of the deed to the shop. La Abuela ducked under the counter—her enormous belly protesting against an action she used to do without thinking—and walked across the shop to open the wooden blinds and unlock the door. The key that always slept in the lock was missing. She spotted it quickly, fallen to the ground in the night. But in the moment when she worried how she'd be able to open the store, she realized that she had lost the word for *key*. And when she found it again, and fit the grimy brass teeth in the lock, she knew that name was no longer right. That name had become a placeholder for the true word still be-ing formed, not only up in the mountains, in the guerrillas' monsoon-and-tobacco-soaked tents, but right there in the dim sewing shop, right on the tip of her tongue.

La Abuela lost words all morning, though she didn't know to connect this shift to the rebels' decision to begin their approach of Campo Chico and encircle the town by the end of the week. She had just lost and found the word for a persistent crease in a collar—though remembering *wrinkle* only revealed the word's new frailty—when the bell above the front door chimed. Polished kitten heels clipped on the rough wood. Two silk parasols rustled and protested at being folded shut. Their carved horn handles clattered against the counter. La Abuela's sisters-in-law. Come to torment her.

Dorotea and Chia—whose names remained inextinguishable as stone, for now at least—waited at the counter. They murmured quietly and spun their silk parasols, to see if La Abuela would emerge at the sound, or if she needed more pointed encouragement. El Papi's daughters never left the house without these parasols, proud of their fair skin that burned at a touch of sun, so they claimed. Since El Papi kicked La Abuela and Benny out of the mansion, Benny's sisters brought their mending to town. There were people at the estate to do the work, but Dorotea and Chia sought the rush of pleasure at seeing La Abuela, their still young, still as-beautiful-as-she-would-get sister-in-law prick her fingers over other people's undergarments.

La Abuela waited in the back room at the ironing board, listening for the pause as the sisters straightened their faces and captured their laughter, the intake before they spoke loud enough that they knew she could hear. The sewing shop had no fan and the only light in the backroom filtered through the blinds in the front. Dust hung in the air and the smell of hot cotton thickened the insides of La Abuela's mouth, making her feel as if she had walked for days without water. She kept the fire for the iron outside, but the wind blew in the wrong direction and smoke always entered the shop. In Campo Chico, no matter how crisp your clothes were, they still smelled of ash.

Chia drummed her fingers on the glass case, but Dorotea was the eldest and more patient. She smoothed her circle skirt, a delicate houndstooth print she'd ordered from the capital, and admired how the shutters cast stripes of filtered light over her open-work lace gloves. She set her face before she spoke and Chia hid her grin behind her hand.

"I heard that the rebels hide so deep in the mountains there isn't any food to eat," Dorotea said. "Just rocks and gravel and dried up bits of wood. With nothing to eat, do you know how they survive, hermanita?"

Chia shook her head.

"They live off food traitors bring them. And *who* would *dare* do such a thing?"

Chia stamped her heel, trying not to burst into laughter.

"The rebels are hideous. They have long, ragged beards and never bathe. The ones camped further down the mountains roam at night and steal the farmers' guns and sugar and grab anything they can get their hands on."

"It's true!" Chia's voice erupted like a bark. "They grab and grab and when they see a woman, they just go crazy!"

"Now, don't get too excited, Chia," Dorotea's voice was glassy. "Save that for your fiancé." Chia flushed and stuck out her lips in a hurt pout. Dorotea cupped her sister's chin in her hand. "Though I'm sure they'd *go crazy*, as you say, over a scrawny half-breed like the one who works here."

The insult was an easy one and Dorotea knew it. She had always called La Abuela what she wanted. La Abuela's mother, Concepción Armando, had been a servant in El Papi's house and died when La Abuela was still very young. Concepción had carried her infant daughter across the island from La Pieza, after Concepción's husband flew to New York and never returned. No one in El Papi's house bothered to remember where Concepción came from, and so La Abuela mourned both her mother and the loss of her story. After Concepción's death, La Abuela slept in the common room—between the nursemaid Ninté's chapped heels and the backs of Abril and Ramona who worked in the kitchens—but spent most of her days with El Papi's children and nephew, learning to read and write. That stopped when a visiting aunt insisted the girl earn her keep instead. Not knowing what else to do, La Abuela copied the older servants' every move, from the kerchiefs they tied around their hair, to their stoop carrying buckets of water, and she learned to talk like them too, bossing around the chickens and lizards in her high, nasally voice, and ordering El Papi's only son Benedicto to steal her fat strips of jerky from the drying racks at the edge of the fields. Dorotea came up with the name "La Abuela" to shame the girl for her boldness, but since the grandmothers in Campo Chico seemed to be the only women that men listened to, La Abuela didn't allow the name to offend. Rather, she grew into it.

"Is anyone back there?" Dorotea called. "Is the shop receiving customers?"

La Abuela finally entered the front room, her arms full of starched sheets and coverlets, which she placed on the counter and began slowly sorting. She stood directly behind the stacks of linen, her swollen belly hidden, knowing that her sisters-in-law came in part to assess how far along she was in her pregnancy. She had thick brows that sharpened her small mouth and a large brown mole in the middle of her cheek. Dorotea explained the order and La Abuela considered words for her sisters-in-law, words that were uncouth and used by the guerrillas and would not need to be remade, words she could pronounce with a practiced crispness no matter how many sewing pins she held in the corner of her lips. The words grew in her, but she waited in silence for the sisters to lose words of their own, or for another quality about them to flicker and fade. She wanted to know the limits and perimeter of this change.

"Maybe our cousin Ignacio will come back to lead the guards," Dorotea said.

Chia rifled through a basket on the counter full of palm-sized silk dolls, each carrying a giant strawberry and stuffed with sand to stick sewing pins in. She flicked one of the doll's black silk pigtails, flinging it out of the basket and across the counter.

"What do you say to that, Chia?" Dorotea nudged her sister ever so slightly, but kept her eyes on La Abuela's face, appraising the effect of her words. "Won't it be wonderful to have our dear Ignacio home?"

"Yes, wonderful," Chia said, and flicked another doll.

La Abuela snatched the parcel from Dorotea's hands.

"I'll have the dresses mended and pressed by Tuesday."

She disappeared back into the ironing room, though she didn't move fast enough to hide that her hands were shaking. Dorotea hadn't even gotten a good look at La Abuela's stomach, though it did seem to be bulging low, a sign that perhaps she carried a boy. She picked up the pincushion her sister had sent rolling and carefully balanced it on the top of the pile. She pressed down on the doll's head with the tip of her nail until it stayed put. A long wait for little reward.

The sisters walked out of the dark shop into the sun and passed a row of old men playing dominoes. The men looked up when the sisters passed, but they did not stand and greet them as they would have even a few weeks before. They simply nodded and placed their chosen pieces of polished bone on the severed tree stump that served as their table, holding their breath until the sisters' parasols were out of sight.

That night La Abuela and Benny lay on their cob mattress in the room above the seamstress's and La Abuela said she was joining the revolution. During their first months in the tiny apartment, the two rooms were stuffed with the useless trappings of a gentleman farmer's beloved son: Benny's evening suits and riding gear, his embossed leather books and baptismal gown. When El Papi kicked them out, La Abuela had insisted on going through each room of the mansion and stacking Benny's trunks in the yard, taking nothing that could be claimed by Dorotea and Chia, but everything that Benny had worn or loved. No one had expected such impetuousness and no one had stopped her. But by the time she said she was joining the revolution, she and Benny had sold everything they could. The rooms bare expanses of plaster and shadow.

"Mi amor," Benny said. "I don't think that's a good idea. It's not safe for the baby."

La Abuela had not been able to hide her second pregnancy from Benny for long. No other part of her body but her stomach grew. Once Benny knew, she refused to wear the loose maternity tunics popular with the women in Campo Chico, nor modify the circle skirts with flouncy crinolines, instead fashioning herself tight, wraparound blouses and pencil skirts, so that from behind she looked exactly as she always had and from the side like she had chosen for some reason to stuff a coconut under her shirt.

"Whose fault is it that I'm pregnant?" La Abuela said. As far as she was concerned the matter of the revolution was settled.

Benny didn't answer. This close to her, he could smell the rose toilette water La Abuela splashed over her face and neck before going downstairs to the shop. He liked her scent best in the early morning before she put anything on. The perfume always made him feel as if he were a child again, waiting in a corner for punishment.

La Abuela peeled the mosquito netting from her bare, sticky legs and turned away. Bright green lizards shifted across the plaster walls she had painted when they moved into the little room, first ash-white in mourning, now deep green for battle. The lizards played in and out of the shadows cast by the curlicues in the wrought iron shutters. She never knew where they came from or where they went. It was a game of hers since her childhood—when she had watched them race across the brocaded wallpaper in El Papi's parlor or the damp stone in the rum cellar—to try to catch one disappearing into the wall, but she never could. She didn't know how they were able to leave without anyone noticing.

Once, when they were children, Ignacio had shown her the scroll where his uncle El Papi kept meticulous record of the family tree, stretching back over the ocean to Galicia and Asturias. Ignacio pointed to his name proudly, but reddened when La Abuela asked why his name was connected to the others in a dotted line and not a solid one. Benny's line to El Papi was two black trunks and Dorotea and Chia each had a solid line of their own. *It doesn't matter*, Ignacio had said, *why don't you try to find your name here,* knowing she couldn't. When she married Benny, a small *m.* was placed by his name, but hers was not added to the scrolls.

"Did my sisters come to the shop today?" Benny propped himself up on his elbow, trying to see La Abuela's face in the dark. "I told them to stay away from you."

A new lizard, this one such a similar dark green to the wall color that it was hard to track, moved in and out of the shadows surrounding the window frame. La Abuela thought of the stacks of ironed cash El Papi kept in his mansion, and of what else was hidden there, what was probably still tucked away in Ignacio's old room. When she and Benny left El Papi's mansion, La Abuela took every letter Ignacio had sent her so that one day, if she needed to, she could use them against him. But after her baby died, she had dreams of the carefully-penned words becoming parts of Ignacio's body, of them crawling from beneath the bed and whispering their truths into Benny's ears. One night the dreams stopped. She reached for the letters and found they had been stolen. A single sheet of the same paper—blank, its watermark elaborate and clear—left in their place so she would know it was Ignacio who had taken them.

Instead of retracing those letters' words, she considered the words she would say to El Papi. Wild words, murderous and world-changing. She imagined the words grew up from the ground beneath the seamstress shop, carried on the backs of termites and those same green lizards, curling round the bedposts and easing through the mattress, to pause in her gut until they made the final journey over her tongue and out her lips. El Papi had always avoided Ignacio's name around her. His eyes flicked to La Abuela and then away whenever his nephew was mentioned. He knew everything that happened in his house.

"After the revolution El Papi won't have any power over us," she said. "And your sisters will have nothing but their scrawny necks to keep their chins so high in the air."

Benny nodded. He knew La Abuela was not the only one saying things like this. He hated his sisters as much as she did. Perhaps, for her sake, he had always hated them more.

There was the island around her. Campo Chico, its tobacco fields, the jungle and mountains, no hint of sea. And there was the island she dreamed of. The revolution would bring her that new island. The rebels would carry new words and carve a path straight to the shore, a path that anyone might walk. Straight to that open palm of green hovering over blue, that soft ground always out of reach. Her home remade.

Two villages east of Campo Chico, a small group of rebels pushed closed the door of an ancient barn. The sunset shone dimly through the wooden slats, narrow strikes that couldn't reach the center of the dirt floor. Desiccated clumps of tobacco leaves hung from the roof beams. The rebels had been ambushed two nights before, half their group slaughtered in their tents, young recruits seventeen- and eighteen-years-old, so fresh from the capital their boots still had soles and laces. The ones who survived were told by a loyal paisano that the landlord in the valley below had seen their fires and ratted them out. The survivors found the landlord and tied him to one of the thick posts that held up his barn.

One guerrilla read the names of the men who had been killed, tripping over their extended patronymics. He had known most of them only a few days. But he repeated the list again and again, asking the landlord if he'd seen the boys, if he knew where they were. He added other names too, of women found strung to lampposts, their limbs twisted and faces slack, of the suspected rebels shot in the street, their eyes blindfolded, yet able to hear the sound of water in the gutters by their house, the rustle of their cousin's pigeons settling in their roost. Soon the names were clear on his tongue, crisp syllables drowning the landlord's whispers.

The rebels stamped their cigarettes into the dirt. The dark heat pressed down on the air outside the barn, choking out all other sounds. The only living people they knew were hundreds of miles away, safe in the capital, or not safe, hiding in crawl spaces beneath floorboards, changing houses each night, waiting to be caught, or already captured and waiting in dark rooms to die, to be thrown into the sea with their hands and feet chopped off. No one would ask the guerrillas what they did that night. No one would know they were there at all.

Tuesday

The ceiling fan was unnecessary, but Ignacio kept it on all day. His office had broad windows with intricate, imported lattices that fractured the light while allowing the capital's sea breeze to pass through. The room was positioned perfectly to be always cool and slightly dark, the fan a luxury unheard of in Campo Chico. Ignacio played an old game with the movement of the fan to comfort himself. By blinking slowly, he tried to capture a still image of the blades instead of the constant blur. To segment something from its whole and indulge in only the parts—to create of it a part. The same green lizards moved across his office walls as in Campo Chico. They seemed more melancholy here against the uncracked walls painted a fashionable gray. In fewer numbers too, as if they survived on the crumbling plaster and manure of which there was so much less in the capital, at least the sections Ignacio frequented. He faced away from the window, leaning back as far as his new leather chair would go to catch the breeze from both the fan and the sea.

El Papi had finally sent him a response that morning. For months, Ignacio had asked his uncle to visit him in the capital. *I will show you a royal time,* he had written El Papi. *Let me repay in some small way all your kindnesses in treating me as your son, as a brother to your children.* The old baron had always refused. Perhaps El Papi knew his name and small fortune meant little in the capital. There, a man's connections to the U.S. mattered, not his land, not his family name, and El Papi's connections were dying out. Perhaps El Papi had sensed this, relayed to him by his ghost pigeons or in Ignacio's boldness of calling during dinner and laughing so loudly El Papi had to hold the receiver away from his ear. Whatever El Papi's reasons for not coming to the capital, Ignacio knew El Papi's motives for keeping him out of Campo Chico. It wasn't just that El Papi had always been fond of La Abuela, with her ironed kerchiefs, her high, nasally voice and pronunciation worthy of the Spanish court, even if the subject was the best method for skinning rabbits or roasting yams. Though family, Ignacio was still a guest in El Papi's house. He had committed a crime of trespass—nothing worthy of vengeance or violence, of course—but still unseemly. Neither called Ignacio's stay in the capital the exile it was. Exile wrapped in a promising government position and a suddenly vacant multiple-story apartment overlooking the sea walk, but exile nonetheless.

Now, however, the rebels were getting closer to Campo Chico and El Papi needed help ordering his band of conscripted peasants. El Papi had increased the village guard from four to twenty men and armed them with Yanqui weapons sent from the capital. But in the towns farther up the mountains the peasants had turned against the guards and slit their throats with machetes normally used to cut sugarcane. They had stuffed the pockets of their guayaberas with the gold fillings from the guard's teeth.

The letter to Ignacio contained no mention of La Abuela, and why should it, the wife of his disowned son, some long-dead servant's daughter? But for Ignacio, it was as if the letters spelling out Campo Chico were always written in her hand, or more accurately, that her body formed the letters, bending and stretching into the landscape of the pathetic village.

He folded El Papi's letter and organized the stacks of documents and envelopes on his desk. He made a list of what he would do to prepare for his absence. Even after all those years, he still felt like he was at the old fool's bidding. But that would change soon. When the rebels lost, those who had fought them would receive special recognition, Ignacio had been assured. His prominence would soon exceed the sugarcane baron's. Many things were possible with that kind of power. He would leave for Campo Chico that day.

La Abuela counted out a quarter of her weekly earnings and placed the bills in an old coffee tin behind the flour.

"Don't forget all the secret spots you're hiding money," Benny said. "You already have a cigar box for the baby under the bed."

"This isn't for the baby," La Abuela said.

"Saving up to buy me something?" he teased.

"It's for the rebels. I learned today that they're coming to Campo Chico. They'll be here Friday or Saturday at the latest."

"Are you sure? It's already Tuesday."

"I know. I will bring it to them as soon as I can."

Benny held his smile, but the money in the coffee tin was too much for even him to bear.

"This year you have made many statements," he said finally.

La Abuela poured a small brown paper bag of rice onto the table and began sorting through the grain for gravel and chaff.

"True."

"All the people in town told me not to believe your pronouncements," Benny continued. "That they were a woman's caprices and would soon pass. But I, who know you better than anyone, knew better."

"Yes, mi amor."

"First you told me to quit smoking because you said it was bad for my health."

"And I was right, you see?" La Abuela pointed to her round stomach. "Besides, all the old folks who smoke sound like their lungs are wells with rats trapped inside them."

"All of them drink, play dominoes, and go to church, should I give those up too?"

"Maybe the church." La Abuela licked her thumb and plucked a stray wisp of straw from the table. "I don't like that new priest. And don't test me on the dominoes."

She reached in her purse for a slim pamphlet made of cheap red paper and placed it on the edge of the table.

"Have you read this yet?"

"No," Benny said. He pushed the pamphlet away from him, careful to avoid La Abuela's neat piles of rice. The less he read or spoke of the guerrillas—with their scraggly beards and endless factions—the less he would encourage La Abuela. But she had him thinking of those men in the mangroves. She had derailed him from his task once again.

La Abuela finished sorting the rice, swept the grains into a pot, and put it to boil with half an onion and a handful of bay leaves. Outside their window, the sky was splitting itself into green and red. Tiny motes of dust, kicked up from the unpaved road, glowed in the column of twilight like plankton in a clouded sea. She sat back down and picked up the basket where she kept her extra mending.

"Then you made me quit boxing," Benny said, "which I was making good money at and you are the one who made me start."

"I was much younger then and foolish. Now I know better."

"I hope you don't change your mind about every decision you made when you were younger."

Benny kissed her neck and smelled roses. He had first proposed to La Abuela when they were ten—both standing in the bright sun, him holding up jerky stolen from the drying racks, stolen just for her.

She stopped his hands and opened her worn parasol, a hand-me-down from his sisters years ago. "You know I never go back on my word."

Humidity had weakened the parasol's silk and there was a long tear, but she was determined to fix it. When they were kids, Benny used to laugh at how much she cared about that parasol, practicing to be able to twirl it just like his sisters did, weeping when they stole it from her. La Abuela still carried the parasol wherever she went, despite its ragged appearance. *It does the job*, she would say. He might laugh at the parasol, but he thought too of how his sisters chased La Abuela and pinched her brown skin. Benny couldn't remember a time when he didn't love La Abuela, and he couldn't remember when his love was not buttressed and laced by the need to protect her, by the knowledge that no one else would, by the pity that knowledge created. She had nothing her whole life and the little she may seem to have—her body, her will— was always slipping into someone else's hands. Loving her meant being the one person that was not a crucible made to melt and reform, but a doorway through which she might pass, carrying all she desired.

"And now you want to join the revolution," Benny said.

La Abuela stiffened. "I'm not asking you to do anything."

"But *you* wish to do something."

"Yes."

"And you *will* ask something of me?"

Outside the window, a little boy sat on top of the fruit wagon and shouted into his cardboard loudspeaker: *fruta bomba, fruta bomba, fruta bomba*. The light was changing, the stripes of green and red fading.

"I can't stay in this town," he said finally. "I can't stay in a place that shames you."

"What do I care about shame?" La Abuela said, licking a piece of thread and pulling it through a needle.

"If Ignacio comes back, I don't know what I will do," Benny said.

"Don't speak of him, we were only children then—"

"*You* were a child."

"I'm not leaving," she said.

"I can go to New York or Miami," Benny said, as he had said many times before. "I can make us money there."

"I'd rather take El Papi's money. I'd rather take it from him with a bayonet pointed at his chin."

Yes, Benny knew La Abuela was not the only one saying things like this. But she was the only one he had to live with and the only one he believed would actually do what they said.

"I'm staying," La Abuela repeated.

She covered the rice and turned down the flame, then moved the kerosene lamp close enough to be able to see her stitches. Outside their window the effervescent motes had disappeared. The sky seemed to have forgotten that it was ever any color but a hot, dark blue. She hoped her words meant, as they always had, that Benny would stay too.

On the edge of Campo Chico's tobacco fields, the ceiba tree cast a shadow so long the tobacco near it never grew as tall as the rest. A woman walked three times around the tree's base, her body a blur in the twilight, and dropped a coin in a small depression in the dirt. The coins clinked against the ones already placed there and rustled up the scent of metal turning to green and flaking to earth. A zunzuncito, the smallest bird in the world, flew across the fields and stopped in front of the woman's chest, hovering in the air as if on a string, its iridescent green body catching the last of the light. The hummingbird was drawn to the strings of cowries and polished red seed beads the woman wore around her neck and to the gold medallion pressed to her skin. The woman held her breath to make the bird stay, but she was not a flower and the zunzuncito disappeared back into the forest. In the lowest branches were molding candles, set there when the tree was young. When lit, they looked like animal eyes, floating in the night.

Wednesday

The next afternoon, La Abuela reached for her mended parasol and descended through the shop out into the market. Fearing either the rebels or the guards, only half of the stands were open. La Abuela walked by a shirtless boy with a distended belly who sold live pigeons. His sister, seated on the wicker baskets filled with birds, her toes curled around the dirty cage floors, collected pesos in a faded red handkerchief tied around her waist. Behind them, the wind moved through the tobacco fields, bending back the leaves, its path through the valley clear.

At the other end of the street, leaning next to a fruit stand, La Abuela saw Ignacio. His posture, at once pompous and failed, was unlike anyone else's in Campo Chico. He must have known she would come to the market, all the women in Campo Chico did, and he was at the stand that sold her favorite fruit. Even across the market, La Abuela could see him slowly stroking a mango's green flesh. She knew his performance was for her alone, repeated until she appeared; he believed he could call her to him. But she would not let him see her. To speak to him and then not tell Benny would be a lie and she already held too many. Ignacio could be anyone, really, from this distance, though she had known the moment he stepped into Campo Chico. That morning she'd woken on the edge of knowledge and when she cracked the orange-yolked eggs into a pan for breakfast it was as if a separate layer of skin had poured over her. The layer was doubly reflective—projecting her movements both to the world and to herself. The layer made it abundantly clear she was not in control of her actions. For the rest of the day, she watched herself: making coffee, stacking the brown paper packages of finished orders for costumers, crouching behind the pigeon cages when Ignacio walked by. The pigeon boy stood beside her, held the largest bird, the one he wouldn't sell, out in front of him, its white wings flapping against his hands. La Abuela felt like a creature in a storybook, thumbed over by many hands.

Outside of the slaughterhouse of Campo Chico, two old women sat, straining their eyes against the horizon in search of clouds. Thin strips of bull and oxen meat hung on racks in the drying fields, desiccating slowly to jerky under the sun. If any storms were sighted, the women would call the workers out of the slaughterhouse to bring the meat in as quickly as possible. They played cards while they waited, their deck as soft as the printed cotton of their skirts, coated with their fingertips' oil. Each card had a mark on the top left corner for what it meant when they weren't playing a game, for the fortune it created when collected in the right hands. A wind came up from the campo and stirred the browning meat, a hot slap like opening an oven door, but there were no clouds yet.

La Abuela was able to avoid Ignacio at the market, but when she returned to the shop after sunset he slipped into the doorway behind her.

"I came home to protect what's mine," he said. "But I see I've already failed. Little Benny managed this all by himself? Didn't need any help from me?"

Ignacio's hand wrapped around her mouth and La Abuela left her body. It was always like this with him. As a child, she had watched her body be carved into a thin sliver of pleasure, knowing she had no choice, and choosing to enjoy. When she'd tried to stop him, it hadn't mattered.

Ignacio pressed against her, pushing her into the narrow doorway. La Abuela bit hard into his palm, at a clump of flesh she could catch between her teeth. But it was a sound behind them that made him pull away. Two women appeared on the road, their white dresses and headscarves glowing in the dusk. One carried a rooster by its feet and the carcass swung with the rhythm of her steps. Ignacio sucked on his hand where La Abuela had bit him. He stared at the passing women and spit blood into the dirt. La Abuela opened the shop door and slipped inside, quickly turning the lock. She could hear him breathing on the other side of the thin wood, then make his way into the street. All someone else's words. No part of her life her own.

Thursday

El Papi enforced a curfew the next day. He did so out of instinct. He did not know—his spies poorly placed or already turned—that the rebels were camped in the mountains outside of Campo Chico. Under El Papi's new curfew, no one could leave the town unless his guards approved and they wouldn't approve anyone they didn't like. Benny couldn't go to New York or Miami now no matter what La Abuela said.

That night, La Abuela walked out of the house, carrying nothing but the bills from the old coffee tin pinned inside her bra. El Papi's guards stopped her before she passed the royal palms that bordered Campo Chico. When she wouldn't turn back on her own, they grabbed her elbows and dragged her to the shop.

Benny opened the door, wearing only his loose, worn underwear. He accepted La Abuela into his arms without a word, receiving her before the guards let her go. Above them a nightjar woke and made its call like the sound of two wooden spoons clapping together. Benny could not sleep, knowing she would try to run again.

Friday

"We're going to make the delivery tonight," La Abuela said, looking up from her mending at Benny.

Beneath their window, a group of boys kicked a rag ball down the street. One of them accidentally sent the ball to the feet of a guard standing in front of the church. The guard kicked it back, right to the boy, but the boy turned and ran, leaving the ball in the dirt.

"Oh, a delivery," Benny said, forcing a laugh he hoped

sounded both sarcastic and unworried. "Gracias a Dios. And who are we bringing this blessed delivery to?"

"To the mountains. Just some food."

"We don't have any food."

"We'll get it. We'll get it from El Papi."

"And what about his guards, mi amor?" Benny pinched the bridge of his nose. He didn't really want an answer.

"No one will stop us in one of El Papi's cars."

"I'm not going in that house," Benny said.

"Everything there should be yours. It should be mine too. I cleaned floors and scraped wax and scoured bed pans for years and so did my mother. Besides, Ignacio won't be there."

From a few well-placed questions of her customers, La Abuela knew Ignacio was staying at the guard's headquarters. She had not told Benny she had seen him. She had not sought Ignacio out and she had not spoken to him. His appearance at the doorway of the shop was too similar to his other visits. Nothing had happened other than reliving all she wanted to forget and she did not tell Benny about every time she remembered something she did not wish to.

La Abuela put down her mending. Perhaps she was pushing Benny too far. But she had no choice. She needed El Papi's money for the rebels and she needed the letters she hoped would still be in Ignacio's old room. She had to get inside that mansion. She had to reach the rebels. She had to try for that island she dreamed of. And she had to know, now, if Benny would join her.

The boys playing football had run inside or into courtyards that swallowed their shouts. The only sound from the window was the guards striking matches and tossing them into the dirt.

"Stay home," Benny said. "The rebels will win or not win without you."

"We'll go tonight," she said, like she was asking for jerky from the drying fields. "Before the rain starts."

The leaves of the ceiba tree had turned inside out, presenting their white underbellies to the darkening sky. Leaning against the wind, the widows of Campo Chico held onto their black lace shawls with one hand and with the other carried inside the vases of lilies that lined the steps into the church. The light melted around them and the dirt roads turned a deeper red than before.

El Papi's tobacco fields came right up to the back of his mansion. He could always see them, even at night, even when nothing was growing. The palm trees shook and salt from the growing storm thickened the air. When Benny and La Abuela came to El Papi's door the rain had just started.

La Abuela slipped behind Benny, moving away from the porch.

"Where are you going?" he asked.

"You knock. If he won't let you in, I can find another way."

"You can't stay out here."

"I know how to get into this house without anyone knowing even better than I know how to get out of it."

"He won't let me in."

"Just try."

La Abuela kissed Benny on the cheek and tucked her parasol behind the porch steps. She disappeared into the thick vines covering the mansion, folding into them as if she was made of them, as if they were welcoming her back into their arms.

Lorenzo, the butler, opened the door and let Benny in without question, like he had been expecting him. El Papi was standing in the parlor looking out over his tobacco. He handed Benny rum in a crystal glass. Clean-shaven, El Papi was lean and tall with muscles like strips of woven hemp. He was dressed in white, his face pale from the hat he wore surveying the fields. But his hands were darker than Benny's, their speckles and sagging flesh the only apparent hint at his mortality.

"She's pregnant again," Benny said, not knowing where to begin or how much La Abuela would want him to say.

"I have eyes," El Papi said. "Is that why you came?"

Benny didn't answer. He hadn't been in his father's house since their first child died, since El Papi told La Abuela never to enter his house again, told Benny that if he left with her the same held for him.

"I think she's scared," Benny said.

"Now that girl decides to be scared. Of what, if you know?"

"Of what will happen if the rebels win."

"They won't, Benny. As much as she might want it. Or thinks she wants it. The rebels are animals. This is the first time they've been outside their pigpen. They think they've discovered a new world, but they've only reached where the slop is made."

"They're winning," Benny said.

"The Americans will stop that."

"Their president supports them."

"But their companies don't. How far along is she?"

Benny never understood why it was after their child's death that El Papi cast them out, instead of after their marriage, or after La Abuela's pregnancy became obvious. Perhaps it was because the little girl's death had broken El Papi's heart too. Perhaps another reason. His father's heart unnavigable to him.

"I won't beg," Benny said and set down his glass. El

Papi turned from him to watch the rain come over his tobacco fields. He nodded slowly, as if not to his son, but to words spoken by something neither of them could make out in the dark.

At the other end of the mansion, Ninté put Dorotea's children to sleep. She had worked as a nursemaid for El Papi's family all her life, had cared even for La Abuela, teaching her how to sew, how to keep her hair clean during the week. Ninté lowered the children onto the thin summer blankets and closed mosquito netting around their four-poster bed. Dorotea watched at the doorway. Her children's limbs shone where the hall light hit and disappeared into shadow where it did not. Dorotea knew that her children were more Ninté's than her own. Ninté had given them more of her body and for longer. That was why Dorotea never spoke Ninté's name. Dorotea knew the other woman's power—at least a portion of it—too well.

Dorotea walked down the hall to Chia's room. Her entrance surprised her younger sister and Chia dropped the wineglass in her hand and it shattered on the wood floor. Dorotea bent to pick up the glass, but then stopped, crouched low, as if suddenly remembering something. The shattered crystal had sprayed all over the room and even dug its way into the thick carpet around Chia's bed, like carcasses of small fish sinking to the ocean's floor, like rodents snatching what they wished and disappearing, never to be seen again.

Unasked, Ninté entered the room and blew out the lamp.

"Listen to that," she said.

The three stood waiting in the dark. Thunder outside and gunshots in the mountains, the two sounds made more similar by the blending force of rain.

La Abuela entered El Papi's mansion through a small passageway used only by the kitchen staff. She crept into the cellar where the wines and rums were aged. El Papi had a good collection and she relished the thought of the rebels toasting with his finest rum. The cellar was where she used to hide as a child from Ignacio. They had played there first when she would let him find her. Later, when she did not want to be found she chose that same place, thinking he would not expect her to go there again.

Climbing back up the stairs with three bottles of ancient rum in her hands, La Abuela saw no one, but she wasn't finished. She headed towards Ignacio's old room. She hoped she had some time. El Papi wanted Benny back, but he didn't know if he had to take La Abuela too, if Benny would come without her, or what would change when the baby was born. El Papi might talk for a long time, testing Benny, testing how far he could be pushed.

In Ignacio's room, La Abuela set down the rum bottles and peeled the heavy carpet off the floor just enough to reveal the hiding place Ignacio had used since childhood. In her mourning, she had sought only peace and she didn't try to get the letters back from Ignacio. But she was no longer mourning. And she realized she'd been a fool; the letters would hurt only her and not Ignacio. Benny knew what Ignacio had done when they were children, but he did not know how long his violence had lasted. La Abuela could not let Benny learn that her marriage vows had been broken for her.

La Abuela stiffened at the sound of footsteps behind her, muffled by the rain and El Papi's plush carpets. She reached for one of the rum bottles and gripped it by the neck. She would crack the bottle across Ignacio's skull, she would not let him touch her again. But when she turned around it was only Chia in the doorway, holding pieces of a broken crystal in her hand.

In that same room, when they were children, Dorotea had held La Abuela's arms behind her back while Ignacio stared into the mirror above his dresser. *That's what I really look like,* he said, pointing to the thin band of skin kept covered by his hat, a white that gleamed like an orchid stem growing under leaves. *That's what color I'd be if it weren't for the sun.* And Dorotea had twisted La Abuela's wrists to compare her skin with theirs, to prove why she must do as they said. La Abuela had never before wondered where Chia was when this was happening, or if they sought her out when they couldn't find La Abuela.

Chia barely reacted at seeing La Abuela crouched in Ignacio's old room, though they were both surprised to find that beneath the stack of letters was a single key, stuck in a crack in the floor beams. Chia's eyes hovered for a moment on the key, guessing at what it opened. But even when La Abuela stood and walked past her, out Ignacio's room and down the long hallway, she said nothing, just followed La Abuela silently, her hand cradling the shattered crystal held away from her body like an offering.

In the center of El Papi's foyer was a large credenza, edged in gold, its drawers locked. La Abuela knew the key she'd found in Ignacio's room opened the top drawer. El Papi, always so proud of the loyalty of those in his house, in the town he owned, kept his cash steps from the front door, within easy reach of anyone with the key or a hatchet. Even from the capital, Ignacio had kept his escape routes well-maintained.

The stuck drawer shook the credenza when La Abuela opened it. The stacks of bills inside smelled like the ironing board in her sewing shop. Hot cotton and ash, the closed room she was leaving.

Down the hall, past the half-open parlor door, El Papi said her name, not to her, but to Benny, and not the name Dorotea had given her, but her real one. The credenza shook again when La Abuela closed the drawer and rattled the cut-glass bowl that had sat atop it for years. She placed her fingers on the rim of the ringing crystal to stop the sound and tucked the money and the letters into her shirt.

Beneath the stand of magnolias outside Campo Chico, a group of rebels crouched in the mud. They shared a hand-rolled cigarette between them, carefully cupping it against the wind and the droplets that broke on the magnolia's over-lapping, waxy leaves. They heard a rustle in the underbrush and reached for their guns, but it was only the little boy who sold pigeons in the market and carried messages for them. They let him have the final puff of their cigarette while they read the news he'd brought. Most of the guards, including that new officer sent in from the capital, were asleep in their bunks. No one in Campo Chico had ratted them out. No one knew they were coming.

"Cariña," Benny said when La Abuela stepped into the parlor. "Papa and I, we've been talking. There's a plane in a few days that will take us to Miami. We can wait there until this thing with the rebels is sorted out. Then we can come home. All of us. It will be alright."

Benny reached out to touch her hand and saw her ragged breath, the thin film of sweat on her forehead, the rect-angular bulk tucked under her shirt.

"I will tell Dorotea and Chia when the plane arrives," El Papi said. "I don't want to give them time to pack. The plane has seats for everyone in this house. No more. My nephew will stay at his post."

He turned from the window to La Abuela. "Come home," he said to her. "Let me finally call you daughter."

La Abuela had all her words planned. Born in the ground and carried through the sewing shop's riddled wood, they had churned in her dreams for weeks. She had held them tight behind her teeth when she exhaled, careful not to let them spill before their time. In the little room above the sewing shop, with only the lizards and peeling plaster as her audience, the words had sounded hollow. But when she finally spoke them in El Papi's house she knew that for all their stilted grandiosity, they were true. Her words were not special, would bring nothing to action, they were not a spell. She was merely picking up a stitch of the whole of what would happen, was already happening, the newness about to be made.

"I will never be your daughter," La Abuela said. "But my child will live and he will be a child of the heroes of the revolution. When the rebels come to cut out your tongue, I will cheer."

El Papi sighed and turned to Benny. "Hijo, please, come with us. You don't have to listen to her."

But Benny had made his decision long ago. Long before his father made them leave, long before he read the letters La Abuela had hidden beneath their bed, the letters he knew she carried now. Before love, before pity, Benny had known that what La Abuela needed protecting from most was his own family.

"I'm sorry," Benny said. "You know I always do what she asks."

El Papi followed Benny and La Abuela down the hall, but turned away when they reached the porch steps. The rain splattered across the open doorway and over the back of his suit, so that the linen darkened and clung to his skin.

Beneath the porch, the almiqui rodent, whose saliva is venomous and whose kind had not been catalogued by scientists for over a century, scuttled out of the ground. No one could hear its movements above the rain. Its scaled tail brushed past La Abuela's forgotten parasol, then curled around its body, thick brown fur bristled against the storm. The almiqui sniffed the air with its crochet-needle nose, smelling beetles and rotting magnolia blossoms and wet dirt. The ceiba trees surrounding the tobacco fields glowed white from their upturned leaves. Any candle lit beneath their branches had been quickly extinguished by the first breath of rain. The racks of drying jerky had been pulled inside. Throughout the campo, everyone had stopped whatever they'd been doing before the storm started. All they could do was stand on their porches and watch the light change, track the palm fronds as they blew across the fields, until even that form of waiting became dangerous.

La Abuela's words were true. The rebels would storm through El Papi's mansion, they would shatter the crystal and make bonfires in the living room from the imported furniture. The horsehair cushions would burn quickly in lashing bursts and make the younger soldiers cry out in fear. Fire-blackened curtains would billow out the windows. When the hurricanes came in the fall, there would be nothing to stop the rain from entering the parlor and bedrooms. The gilded wallpaper would mold. Water lemon vines would waltz down the hall.

The almiqui didn't mind being wet, but its home was in the dirt. Uncaring of La Abuela's steps above, it took a few more careful sniffs of the green air. It caught—with a five-fingered, sharp-clawed paw—a cicada, plump and pale in new skin. The revolution would reshape the almiqui's life too, or at least the life of its species. First, by destroying thousands of acres of jungle to make way for sugarcane; then, when that economy collapsed, by leaving other swaths untouched; until finally, decades later, the almiqui will be rediscovered by humans and deemed—along with the Zapata Wren, the Least Tern, the Evening Bat and dozens of others—something worth protecting.

Perhaps, if the almiqui wanted, it too could speak. Of El Papi's carefully-constructed lineages, those scrolls unrolled and inked into at each new birth, of what the revolution would bring, imaginable and not, if it would give the island La Abuela dreamed of back to her or unfurl another place entirely. Surely in no known language, in no letters ever printed, but in some arcane tongue, the almiqui might have one word, just one, to spit into the dirt. But the animal dug its way back into the earth beneath the porch of the mansion. It needed nothing more above ground.

La Abuela and Benny reached the edge of the porch, then walked in the rain to one of El Papi's cars. In the passenger seat, she tucked Ignacio's letters more firmly behind the parcel of cash, and smoothed her blouse to cover them both. No matter what the rebels brought, La Abuela couldn't live with the idea of anyone else reading the letters. Or of the words still existing, even if they remained unread. She would burn the letters the first chance she got and it would be the letters' words that were forgotten, that were lost to smoke, not ordinary words like *wrinkle* and *key*. She and Benny would go into the mountains. She would leave no trail to follow her by.

THE ELEPHANT'S FOOT

I first saw the elephant's foot on the cement run outside of chapel. Muirenn was jumping rope, her body so steady her wool skirt barely floated above her knees, inching closer to Sandra's Double Dutch record. I counted under my breath, letting the numbers shape fully in my mind and over my tongue. I didn't like to say them out loud, but pretended instead they were a secret to myself. They were simple numbers, but all numbers were simple and they all could be twisted into something strange. In my pocket I ran my fingers over Muirenn's study cards with the presidents' names on them, right up to our beloved, newly-elected John Fitzgerald Kennedy, who the nuns had us pray for and who everyone in school claimed to be related to but me. Muirenn had covered his card in red hearts. Whenever she jumped, Muirenn asked me to hold her cards. She said I gave her luck.

"Twenty-five, twenty-six!" the girls around us called.

It was cold, November, and cloudy enough to almost want a streetlight, even in mid-morning. Sandra and the other girls chanted to the swat of the rope hitting cement. Sandra had always been the biggest in our group and the leader. But she wasn't going to be the prettiest. It might be Muirenn, or even—if I stayed out of the sun and started waking up early to straighten my hair—me.

"Twenty-seven! Twenty-ei—"

"Touch!" Sandra yelled and the spinning stopped. "I saw Muirenn touch the rope."

"I did not," Muirenn said, staring hard at Sandra's knees. The rope lay tangled between her shoes.

"Louisa saw it too," Sandra said.

Louisa was short and kind of dirty, not pretty, not smart. Her father worked for a butcher on Damen Avenue and they lived in the tiny apartment above the shop. Sandra liked to tell her she smelled of meat. It was true, especially after her mother died. Not like something cooking, but the raw scent of pink pieces of chicken or dark blood sausage.

"I don't know," Louisa said. "Maybe—"

Sandra shoved Louisa and she fell back onto the cement. She didn't even try to catch her fall, just curled tight around her satchel like it held something precious.

"Do over," Sandra said. "You get one more chance."

We started counting, all the way back at the beginning.

It was Muirenn who'd first spoken to me, her perfect oval face circled by burnt-orange curls that never frizzed or tangled, skin white as the statue of St. Bridget that greeted us at the front door. When I first came to St. Bridget's All Girls Prep, I was still learning English, though I learned fast. My name sounded so foreign in the nun's mouths I didn't even think it was mine. *CEC-il-a Arm-and-dough.* Muirenn called me *Ceely* instead and asked if I wouldn't come sit by her and her friends. If I wanted to study in her silent, clean kitchen while I waited for my sister to take me on the Red Line back to the South Side.

"Eight, nine, ten!"

Sandra's voice drowned everyone else out. I counted in my head and I rooted for Muirenn, but silently.

"Eleven, twelve!"

Louisa poked me between the shoulder blades. "Want

to see something?"

I shrugged her off, my eyes never leaving Muirenn's dancing feet.

"It's a secret," Louisa said. "I'm not going to show anyone else."

I knew that was a lie. Last summer, Louisa had found a Ouija board and coaxed us to her apartment above the butcher's, promising we could stay as long as we wanted. It was much better than the other spirit-calling games we'd played—Rap on the Table or Ghost at the Window. But Sandra said we'd be punished if we got caught. We pricked our fingers with embroidery needles and swore loyalty to each other and loyalty to Sandra above all. It was hard to get the needle to draw any blood, but when it did, we each squeezed a drop onto Sandra's upturned palm. She closed her fist to mix the blood, we pressed our thumbs back on her palm, and brought them, stained, to our mouths. Our oath wasn't something we talked about, but whenever I'd think of going against Sandra, my index finger touched my thumb and I wouldn't.

I knew Louisa would tell Sandra, eventually at least. But I liked the idea of a secret—even if it was only mine for a moment.

"Come on, Ceely," Louisa said.

After a summer of going to Louisa's every afternoon, slipping past the silver hooks waiting for meat, the tubs of blood congealing in the cooler, Louisa's dad had found us with the Ouija board and chased us out of his apartment. Louisa said that after we were gone, he broke the board in half and hit her across the backside with it. We hadn't dared to play since. Really, we were less shaken by being found with the outlawed game and more by what her dad had almost caught us doing. At night in bed, I'd stare at the picture of La Caridad del Cobre above me—her robes blue as the sea she appeared out of, the three boys in their little boat who she steered back to the island—and I'd wonder if the nuns had been right. If the devil we'd called with the board had gotten inside us, had been the one to make us kneel and kiss just to see how it felt and then switch to see who kissed better. We stayed as far apart as we could, necks craning in, only our closed mouths touching. One playing boy, the other playing girl. Pairing off and taking notes, the taste of each, the shape of lips. Because if the devil had gotten in us, I didn't know the difference. I couldn't tell him apart from my own thoughts, what I'd already wanted. I didn't know if I cared.

"Ceely!" Louisa poked me again between the shoulder blades, harder this time. "Come here."

"Fine, I'll look," I said.

The girls were all watching the Double Dutch. Across the road, the boys we might be mixed together with next year in high school played basketball, two sets of chain link fence between us. Louisa made me step away from the group and though we were right in the middle of the playground, it felt lonely. The wind whipped around us, tossing up Louisa's stringy braids, pulling the wisps behind her bangs out and into the air.

"Come closer," Louisa said.

She unbuckled the clasp of her bag. She had one of those plaid satchels, purple and brown with a gold clasp like we'd all begged for, though Louisa had been the last to get it. The sisters of St. Bridget's were always threatening to make the bags illegal because they were a vanity. Books could be held in your hands and more than books could be hidden in bags.

"You've got to swear not to tell," she said.

There was something new and fierce about Louisa. She'd never given me an order before. It was as if she didn't care what I did—and that made me want to listen. I made an *x* over my heart and eyes, the slap of the rope keeping beat in my head. I thought of the names Sandra called Louisa, or when she'd shove her or smack her into a wall. Louisa's face afterwards was as hard and lifeless as the polished stone of the chapel altar.

I crouched against the wind and pressed closer to Louisa's satchel. For a second all I could see was dark, until a shape began to form. In the bottom of her bag was something large, round, and heavy. It looked kind of shriveled, like a big, forgotten-about potato.

"That's all your dad would give you for lunch?" I said.

"Look closer."

She brought the bag up to my face and soon I could see that the wrinkles were in thick lines, rather than puckered the way a potato got. They looked like the stockings of the women praying in mass, bunched and crumpled at the ankle, old-feeling. At the base was something smooth and black.

The Double Dutch numbers stopped in my head. I took my fingers off Muirenn's study cards. I didn't feel cold anymore.

"What is it?" I whispered.

Louisa smiled. "It's an elephant's foot," she said. "It can tell the future."

I knew exactly when Louisa showed Muirenn. Louisa followed Muirenn to the bathroom before French and afterwards Muirenn didn't raise her hand or open any of my notes for the rest of class. Usually, Muirenn always answered each question so perfectly that the nuns said she was destined to join their ranks. Muirenn prayed constantly—before meals, before tests, before she made any decision, no matter how small. Put her little hands together and tightened her lips into a frown. But she'd told me that she'd never once actually heard His voice. I hadn't either. My head swirled with so many things: the nun's whispers in English and Latin, my mother's Spanish that even then I knew I was forgetting, my own wants and fears. But no sound as strong and pure as I thought His voice or even the voice of one of His saints might be.

For the rest of French, Louisa's bag was on the floor by her desk. Muirenn kept turning around in her seat to look at it. Our eyes locked when she caught me staring. Sister Agnes rapped on Muirenn's head with her knuckles and told her to pay attention.

Sandra knew something was happening by lunchtime. All day Muirenn and I had been looking at her funny, then looking at each other. We were waiting for Sandra to act. When she did nothing, we got itchy, but we liked it too, knowing something she didn't.

"What's the matter with you all?" Sandra said.

We sat silent until Muirenn could no longer take it.

"Louisa has something to show you," Muirenn started to say, but Louisa reached across the cafeteria table and knocked her water glass all over Muirenn's food. Muirenn stood up, breathing heavily through her nostrils, the stain from the water spreading over the lap of her dark wool skirt.

Muirenn shouted, but I grabbed her hand to calm her. *Let Louisa win this*, I tried to say with my fingers pressed firmly into her palm, *Let's see what she does next.* Across from us, Louisa sat completely still, not even looking at Muirenn, her eyes on Sandra instead.

"Fine," Sandra said. "Keep your stupid secret."

She shoved away from the table and Louisa grabbed her bag and hurried after her. I thought I could see the shape of the foot pressing against the fabric. Just before they rounded the corner and disappeared from view, Louisa slipped her arm into Sandra's, and leaned her lips close to Sandra's ear.

After that, we talked about nothing but the elephant's foot. Every chance we got, Muirenn, Sandra, and I sat across from Louisa like the nuns did when they brought you in for a grilling in the Mother Superior's office. Each of us felt we had a fuller knowledge of it than anyone else.

Louisa's story of how she got the elephant foot would change depending on who she was telling it to. She told Muirenn the foot came from her great uncle, who died working for the British Royal Indian Guard, and sent the foot to their shop wrapped in the Union Jack. When her father saw the flag, he tossed the whole package in the fire, but Louisa scooped it out when he wasn't looking.

She told me the elephant foot had belonged to a distant cousin who flew all around the world in a balloon and was in love with Louisa's mother. The cousin gave the foot to Louisa's mother to try to stop her from marrying Louisa's dad. That didn't work, but before Louisa's mother died, she gave the foot to Louisa, and told her not to tell anyone.

When we confronted Louisa about these alternate stories, she would blink at us and toss out another lie. Or she'd stay silent until we were mad enough to hit her and then whisper the one line from every story that never changed: *It can tell the future.*

We gathered facts as best we could. Muirenn figured the foot was too small to belong to an adult, so it had to come from a baby elephant. Louisa said that the foot was carved by hunters from the belly of a murdered elephant mother, before the baby was even born. She said that when an animal is killed, all of its energy and knowledge goes into whatever part is chopped off first, and since elephants are incredibly wise, there was a lot of stuff in that foot. She told us that baby elephants can cast terrible curses.

"Just tell us where it's really from," Sandra said when we were putting on our coats for recess.

"From the deepest, darkest Africa," Louisa said in a practiced, dramatic voice. "From the wildest jungles where not even missionaries dare go."

"Maybe it's related to Ceely then," Sandra said.

I zipped up my coat and turned away, so they wouldn't see the blood rushing to my face.

"Maybe you should study geography better," Muirenn said. "There's no elephants in Cuba."

"Maybe I should smack you," Sandra said. She hadn't threatened Muirenn or me in years. She had no need. Unlike with Louisa, she only had to hurt us once and we remembered. But since Louisa had shown us the elephant foot, we weren't as afraid of Sandra as before.

"I was just teasing," Muirenn said, though she didn't look down.

"I'm bored with this stupid game," Sandra said. "Let's go outside. I bet you'll never beat my record, Muirenn."

On the cold cement, we jumped rope and counted, but only half-heartedly, thinking about the wrinkled skin, the small curved nails hidden in the bottom of Louisa's bag.

There was a special strangeness to the foot. Even if we didn't believe Louisa, we believed in the foot. It made Muirenn and me quiet around it. It made Sandra something else.

One day, I was in the bathroom washing up and Louisa was in a stall. She'd brought her bag in with her, of course. She wouldn't leave it out by the sink and ask one of us to watch it like everyone else. I figured she'd hung the bag up on the hook inside the stall, and I couldn't stop staring at the door reflected in the mirror. The fabric must be stretching from the weight of the foot. The longer I stared, the more I thought the door was pulsing.

Sandra entered the bathroom, awkward up on her tiptoes and her shoulders crouched. "Where's Louisa?" she whispered.

I gestured behind me with my chin. I don't know why I didn't say something out loud—I was staring too hard at the door. Sandra smoothed down her hair and kicked hard at the stall. The little metal latch broke, fell to the tile, and skittered across the floor. Louisa was sitting on the toilet, her satchel on her lap.

"Give me the bag, Louisa."

Louisa didn't say a word, just stared, first at Sandra, then at me. Sandra tried to yank the bag away, but Louisa held tight.

"Do you see this, Ceely?" Sandra said to me. "Louisa won't listen."

I nodded. Sandra saying my name meant I couldn't leave.

Sandra knelt down slowly in front of Louisa. She wrapped her fingers around Louisa's ankle.

"Go on, Louisa," she said, softly, as if she was asking. "I just want to see your bag."

I thought about our oath to each other. Touched my thumb as if I could still feel where I'd pricked it. Sandra brought her hand higher up Louisa's leg, flattening it like a ruler, then slipped her hand just under the hem of Louisa's skirt and held it there.

"Give it to me."

"No," Louisa said.

I counted the seconds Sandra held her hand, unmoving but tense, on Louisa's thigh—*eleven, twelve, thirteen.* Finally, Sandra shoved Louisa sideways and though Louisa banged against the metal wall, she still didn't speak. Sandra stood up, pushed out of the stall, and left the room without even glancing at me. Louisa sat on the toilet, shaking, her face red. The whole time she didn't let go of her bag.

I tried to tell Muirenn what happened in the bathroom, but I couldn't get the words right.

"She did what?" Muirenn asked.

"Sandra, she put her hand under—"

"She did not."

"She did. I saw it."

"Shut your dirty mouth, Ceely. You're lying."

"I'm not. I swear."

"You are," she said. "You're dirty and you make us do dirty things."

"I'm not the one who—"

I stopped talking. I didn't want to say what we both knew, that it wasn't Sandra, but Muirenn, perfect Muirenn, who had first suggested we kiss in Louisa's apartment, our knees pressed into the prickly carpet.

"The one who what?" Muirenn said.

"If I'm dirty," I said, "then you're dirty too."

Louisa didn't come to school the next day or the day after. The rest of us avoided each other. Sandra played Double Dutch with a group of younger girls and Muirenn ate lunch with Sister Agnes talking about Saint Hildegard or something. No one noticed that I'd ironed my hair flat, though I'd burnt a thin line on my forehead trying to get the hair in front straight. When I thought of the elephant's foot, I saw Sandra's hand creeping up Louisa's leg, pressing into her skin and leaving pink marks, the number of seconds filling my mouth, choking me.

Then, a whole week later, Louisa came back. Her hair was combed and clean and no strands escaped from her tight braids. Her uniform was ironed and the collar starched, the way it had always been when her mother was alive. But her bag was empty. It made me almost sick, how much I wanted to see the elephant's foot. How seeing it was my first thought.

In homeroom, Louisa went up to the board to sharpen her pencil. For years, the four of us had taken seats in a row, to make it easier to pass notes during class. Louisa walked slowly back to her seat and slipped bits of paper from her pocket onto each of our desks. We kept our hands folded. No one looked up.

Each card had a name written on it. The invitations were made of brown butcher paper, a couple of layers pasted together. She'd drawn little flowers with vines coming off of them in different colors around the single phrase: *Learn what your future holds!* On the back was Louisa's address on Damen. The invitations were for that night and they promised her dad would be out late. Muirenn didn't turn around, but I knew she was reading the invitation. The back of her neck turned bright red. I looked behind me and caught Sandra slipping the paper underneath her waistband.

We hadn't been to Louisa's since her dad chased us out for playing Ouija. The store was dark and Louisa opened the locked door with a key. We walked by the empty cases, the light from streetlamps shining on the glass, all the meat brought in for the night.

"So, this is where you got the foot," Sandra said, tapping her fingernails on the display glass. "Your dad's been feeding us elephant parts."

Louisa shook her head and opened the door at the back of the shop that led up to their apartment. "Don't be stupid," she said. "Elephant's too expensive for you."

We followed Louisa, hardly watching our steps up the stairs, staring at her bag because it had once held the foot. The bag bounced up and down on the small of her back.

When we stepped into her apartment, Louisa wouldn't turn on any of the lights. We stumbled through the kitchen and into the sitting room stuffed too full of couches and rockers. Louisa had us all sit on the floor. The light through the greasy windows was dim, making each of us glow. Muirenn smiled at me. In the dark, the room had the sweet, sacred feeling of chapel after dusk, our chins tilted up to practice receiving the host.

"Well, where is it?" Sandra said and slouched back on the couch like she was bored. I thought she pretending, biding her time.

"I'll get the foot," Louisa said. "But you have to close your eyes first."

I kept mine partially open, eyelids fluttering over my nose and looking down. Louisa came into the room, stepping carefully around the chairs, holding a big platter with a cloth over it. The cover was something nice, silky and flowered—probably one of her mom's good scarves.

I caught Muirenn's eyes right before Louisa said we could open them. She looked funny in the light. She didn't wink at me or make a face. She looked back at the platter, waiting.

Louisa uncovered the foot with a flourish. It seemed smaller than it had in Louisa's bag. Dusty and quiet. Almost unimportant. We all glanced at each other, feeling we'd been fooled. But Louisa lit the candle sitting on the platter. In the light, the foot changed. The skin looked older, each wrinkle visible. The foot swelled, like it was alive, like it was breathing. Whatever we were going to say to Louisa gurgled and popped in our throats.

Louisa went back to the kitchen and returned with a pitcher of water.

"According to legend," Louisa said, "the spirit of the dead elephant will speak through a body of water." She took everything off the platter, including the foot, and poured water slowly into it. The platter was silver, or silver-plated, and tarnished, though the nicest thing in the apartment. "But," she continued, "we must be sure to contact it through a body of water small enough to contain it. If the water is too large, the elephant will be able to emerge in the flesh and seek its revenge."

"How will we know what the foot says?" Muirenn asked. "There's no board."

Louisa didn't answer. She picked up the elephant's foot and placed it in the center of the platter.

"What are you doing?" I said. "You'll ruin it."

"This is how it's done," Louisa said.

"But what are the rules?" Muirenn asked. "We have to know the rules first."

Louisa stared at the foot. Its shape reflected in the silver platter, the water still rippling from when Louisa set it down.

"Ceely, you can ask the first question," Louisa whispered.

I could only think of something boring. But since it was probably just Louisa who was going to answer, I asked it anyway.

"Will we get into good high schools this year?"

After I spoke, there was an echo in my head, in a way I couldn't place, like it was my own voice speaking back to me. You can't really hear your own voice, because you've always heard it. It's just words or meaning—not a voice at all. The sound was loud, though I knew it was only inside me. I'd get into Sacred Heart, it said, which was my top choice. I opened my eyes and looked at the others. They'd heard it too, in their own heads, with their own answers. The sound left a sort of scrape in my ears, like chairs across the cafeteria floor, but not fading.

"It told me I'll get into Sacred Heart," Muirenn said.

"It told me the same thing," I said.

"Oh good, we can walk together," Muirenn smiled and grabbed my hand. Her palm was damp and her square-cut nails pressed into my skin.

"It told me that too," Sandra said, though I didn't believe her.

"What'd it tell you, Louisa?" I said.

Louisa looked at the foot and smiled. "It's your turn to ask now, Muirenn."

"Okay," Muirenn said. "Will they make me become a nun? Or will I get married?"

The voice was silent for me, but I could tell from Muirenn's face it had told her something—her face tightened and her gaze drifted inside herself.

"My turn," Sandra said.

"No," Louisa said. "You're going last."

Sandra bristled. I worried that she might hit Louisa or make us stop.

"How come?"

"Because of our oath," Louisa said. "You're the leader. And the leader goes last. To ask the most important question."

"Fine." Sandra slumped against the sofa, satisfied.

"I'll ask now," Louisa said and turned toward the foot. "Will we still be friends next year?"

The voice answered, each our own private response. It was clear from everyone's faces that the answer was no. Muirenn looked at me, her mouth sorry like she was ashamed, not of me, but of herself.

We should have walked away after that question, but we didn't. We went around the circle, each except Sandra asking a question, each getting an answer loud and reverberating like we were inside the church organ at mass, but only in our own heads. Some of the answers we didn't like and we stopped sharing them, asking the questions faster, around and around the circle. When will we marry? Will we be ugly or pretty? How many children will we have? How long will they live? When will our parents die? When will we? Soon the voice was all there was in our heads, the ringing carrying over the questions. Like it was God, finally, inside of us, and it wasn't nice.

I didn't want to keep asking, but I did. Muirenn was crying, but her lips were still moving. The answers weren't something you could live with after hearing them. Like we could just walk out of the apartment and go on. The answers stuck to us. I didn't see how we'd ever leave or how we'd ever stop asking.

"Sandra," Louisa said, her tight, high voice breaking through the sounds in our heads. "It's your turn now. Come with me. The last question gets asked alone."

Louisa picked up the platter, careful not to spill a drop. She walked into the bedroom and Sandra followed, her head down and hands clasped behind her back. She shot me a wolfish smile just before she stepped into Louisa's room. I knew then that she hadn't heard any of the answers, or the sound that ricocheted through our bones since I asked the first question. She still thought it was all a game. The door shut behind them.

"Wait!" Muirenn cried as if she hadn't seen them walk across the room. Her eyes were swollen and her hands shaking. "I need to ask one more question," she shouted. "I wasn't done!"

But no one answered us from inside the bedroom. Through the door, I could hear whispers, then movement. Hands and feet on the floor, cloth on the floor.

"What are they doing in there?" Muirenn shouted. "What's she's asking?"

Sandra whimpered, a sound I'd never heard before. The whimpers turned to a low moan and then she screamed. She screamed again.

There was a clodding sound downstairs, keys dropped and picked up again.

"That's Louisa's dad," I said. "What'll we do?"

From inside the bedroom, I heard a scuffle. The sound of someone getting up, the platter clanging to the floor. Water sloshed onto the wood floor. Muirenn ran to the bedroom door and pulled on the knob, shaking the frame. The door wouldn't budge.

"Let me in," Muirenn yelled. "Let me in!"

I stayed where I was and stared at the door. Muirenn

crouched on her hands and knees trying to see through the keyhole into the bedroom. Water eased out from under the door and reached for her skirt, wetting the wool, wetting her skin. There was so much more water than Louisa had poured. It leaked out from under the bedroom door and gathered in a pool, ready to spread across the room. Muirenn cried out and backed away. I heard Louisa's father stumbling up the stairs, but I kept my eyes on the water. I could see something surfacing slowly, getting bigger and more solid as it rose.

ARE WE EVER OUR OWN

Selected letters between Samantha Maria Armando
Castell and Jack Walldris[1]

On September 7, 1966 Armando Castell wrote to Walldris,
having just obtained his address in Marin County from their
mutual friend, Thomas Boston.

~~Dear~~ Jack,

You say my work is disappearing. Turning in on itself—
getting smaller and smaller. You say "domestic, tidy, craft."
You don't mean "craft" in that nice way the boys upstate
with their forged steel boxes do. You say, "think bigger, bird,

---

1 Though the artists Samantha Maria Armando Castell and Jack
Walldris had known each other since their childhoods together in Houston
and heavily influenced each other's early work, their correspondence is
relatively brief. The surviving letters in the Walldris Estate are limited to
the time when they were arguably the furthest apart, both geographically
and aesthetically. The letters presented here range from September 1966
to September 1967: from directly before Armando Castell's first dated
"womb-island-work" to Walldris's decision to permanently relocate to
California where he founded the conceptual art space: LIGHT/BEing/
LIGHT (LBL). Armando Castell is writing from Manhattan.
Editor's Note: With some exceptions for the sake of clarity, the origi-
nal spelling and punctuation of the letters has been preserved. Finally,
though Armando Castell used various pseudonyms throughout her career
(Samantha Armand, Sam Castle, etc.), I will refer to her as the name she
used before her death: her full name.

think like you are in the sky." Well, you're the one who told me to paint with my cunt.

Thomas tells me you're in California—building something big or "not-building," he kept saying that, "not-building," imitating your fake Brooklyn vowels, consonants deep in your gut-groin (does anyone else but me remember that Texas twang we arrived with?), Thomas's scare quotes getting wider with each gimlet. But I will ask point blank, man-like, I will ask why I had to hear from Thomas crumpled over his regular barstool at Danny's that you were making something big in California? You'd gotten the grant—you're welcome—and off you were, for months, Thomas said, because before you "not-build" you have to unbuild, and that can take a long time, baby. Note the BABY, these too increased with Thomas's gimlets, though I have to say they didn't start with them. You're gone with no expiration date and I'm back to being called "baby" by the likes of Thomas on his barstool. I'm back to being anybody's for the taking. I know you like Thomas. Shit, you even like his paintings. And I know how it sounds—desperate, clingy—but I don't care : did you forget my number and where I worked and where I lived and where all my friends work and live, who are your friends too, including Thomas, who knew where you were, so I guess you didn't? I would have loved to come back from downtown at 2 in the morning and smudge my hand into a big red painting of California on my door. Or an orange. I'm desperate and my art is small, minuscule, crafty, disappearing cloth WOMBS. That's the word. You said it. You're right.

Yours,
Sam

December 7, 1966:

Dear Jack,

Instead of saying "I miss you," I'll say:

I'm sure Thomas already told you—it's like he wrote it in the sky, I've heard it so often from everyone—but you are way out in those trees of yours. Thomas nailed the big opening of your work. Wine and frou-frou and all the Uptowners drooling. (Everyone asking where you were, hoping you'd pop out at the end, even more in awe when you didn't.)

I'm gonna be honest, Jack. I don't know about the stuff. It seems secondhand—not just of one artist or thing-y, that's fine, I like people talking to each other with their sculptures, but the way Thomas set it up especially, it's like you've ripped off the whole <u>right now</u> feeling. Everything you've got in there is selling fast (I'm telling you in case Thomas didn't, in case he's keeping those receipts tight to the chest). But your work is selling because it's <u>exactly</u> what everyone wants. They want it bad. I overheard these late-to-the-game flower-babies trying to pinpoint who you ripped off—they didn't use those terms—but that's the beauty of what you've done. You can't say it's this cat or that cat. Those kids are protesting in the street and getting killed in Vietnam and you give us these perfect metal spheres and cubes, made of iron and steel. They look like bombs, obviously, but, "I'M SORRY" they don't look like them in a bad way, in a <u>critical</u> way. They look like how we <u>want</u> bombs to look : beautiful and powerful, weighing so much they warp the building, they're a danger, sure, but only to the people on the bottom floor. "That's America, man," I say, but Thomas says, "No." He says, "It's not political, it's not personal, it's ART." Boy, do the buyers love hearing that—I mean politics are so messy right now, you know?

With all the money Thomas got from selling your work, he's opening up a new space and he's even got an assistant. In case you care, I said no to that. Some roles are beneath even me.

Are we ever our own,
Sam

February 13, 1967:

The wombs are dark inside, they are inconceivable. I mean bomb static I mean Hiroshima. The outlines of people in white on the walls? What painting could be clearer? How do you paint after that? If it's bodies you are after, they are all around you, one after the other to trace your pencil over. That's my biggest fear. That some asshole, Thomas or whoever, is gonna come up to one of my wombs and just touch it. Then they'll see it for what they think it is—then that's all they'll be able to see of it. Then they'll just have one meaning. That's why I gotta change the name. Not to erase you. That's why, each time I start it's like I've never made one before. I keep having those "first-time" fears. I can't decide on the size. I haven't made anything in months. How can I? Every stitch is too big or too small. I want something I can crawl inside. Disappear in. Make myself an island, sink into its core. I want something no one else can see. How can I be as big as I need to be and as invisible still? I want the wombs to be perfect jewels only I know the making of. Unrecordable / unrecognizable.

Sam

March 12, 1967:

Dear Jack,

Big idea! I've started an exhibition with the WOMBs and photographed them! Photos enclosed, you're welcome. PHOTO#1 is under the bridge right when it was light enough: the womb is in the top right corner, next to the gray rocks. You can't see it, but it's there. PHOTO#2 is on Thomas's barstool at Danny's: note how the brown fabric and ochre thread stand out against the green stool (black and white film, I KNOW, use your imagination). In the background you can just make out V's new plastic-cock-sculpture. PHOTO#3 is mostly dark—I was on the run. Still, I think it's the least successful documentation of my most successful piece. The WOMB is in someone's pocket—a business man in a fedora on the A train. I slipped her in just fine, but the photo was hard—he thought I was trying to get something <u>out</u> of his pocket not trying to photograph something I'd put <u>in</u> it. The estrangement process: me walking away from wombie after insisting that I'd taken nothing from business man. He even checked his pockets and wombie almost fell out and I was afraid I'd lose her to the subway car floor, but she clung on tight. He didn't see her, but she'll be with him a long time. Anyway, I had to walk away from her—my child/creation—and that's where the big focus is, you know? Me walking away from this perfect minuscule womb I've spent days sewing. I'm gonna do it again and again. I like to think of them bumping against people's thighs and loose coins, waiting calmly in the dry cleaner's rack. I like to think of all the fingers they'll touch.

Sam

April 5, 1967:

Dear Jack,

The size thing was a joke, can't take it?[2] And really, that's the first thing you write me? I'll be back to literal—nothing there but what I say. All my <u>Structures</u> are about life-size, you know wombs are actually only as big as a pear. Obviously, THEY CAN STRETCH. And no, I'm not "going nuts without you." I'm joking—in my way, which you know what that means—I'm not really joking. The size, I'm exploring it. I mean it's not a joke. You know I'm not funny.

Even after all these usages, I'm not sure "womb" is the right word—it's still <u>your</u> word. I thought I'd make the label mine, but I'm not sure you picked the right one, bad you. Maybe <u>mouth</u> is better. What's the difference, you say? I'm talking creation, being loud. Again, the difference, you'd ask? Womb/mouth/teethed womb? I keep thinking <u>island</u>, though that doesn't make sense. You want me to get away from the canvas, but I like that containment. It's how I feel, surrounded by water. Even though it isn't true, I still feel like there's a depth between where my body ends, and another, yours, Thomas, whoever's filling that indentation to the left of me in bed, begins. I want to trace that spot, tongue that border, yeah, you say GET OVER IT, but first I have to <u>know</u> it. And I don't always <u>want</u> to be over it. I like my space. I don't always like yours.[3]

---

2 This comment seems to refer to a no longer extant exchange. Though Armando Castell makes reference to Walldris's reticence in communicating with her, it is unclear how many of his letters she herself might have destroyed. Walldris refused to comment on his supposed silence towards Armando Castell.

3 Unsigned.

April 28, 1967:

Jack,

Since we are on the topic, Thomas confirms that your boxes are still selling like hotcakes. (We both make boxes, jaja, but I guess yours are more profitable. Which begs the question, which one of us is turning tricks?) The reflective ones are really good, Thomas says, he's even upped the price. They're so shiny and before the buyer buys one, he leans in and catches a glimpse of the image he wants to see of himself: taut, contained, and powerful, a man made of airplane. I myself prefer the image of my foot getting closer and closer to its own reflection. It hurts to kick your boxes, but I keep doing it.

Sam.

May 1, 1967:

Jack,

I think I'm writing to myself. That's too easy. I'm writing to a you that's been hoisted into me. Second self/mirror self/self just far enough to see. Only my brain knows it's me. My hands don't, they think it's you and that words are the closest thing to touching you. It's like when I'm making my wombs. I know what a womb is, but my hands (doing the making) are stitching and cutting and smoothing out knots—they're purely physical, no ideas. They smell like glue, they're thumbing around in the sticky dark, looking for something sweet. They're enjoying the chase. I want to make these perfect, self-contained structures, empty holes that are impenetrable, structures you can't even see. My tools are so dainty. I went to a sewing shop and said I was embroidering on baby slippers and you should see the things the woman there sold me. Silver glinting teeth and tongues—so sharp. I want to build something so small you can't even see it. I want to put them everywhere and no one will notice.

Sam[4]

June 3, 1967:

Dear Jack,

Thanks for the photos. The package was ripped so I only got the ones of the red rocks with green lichen on them and the one of the dead snake. I like that, can't believe your dog ate it! I keep seeing him with a snake inside him, whole, not slithering around, but like with a new backbone—solid and fixed.

Forwarding you Thomas's gimlet bill. To burn or film?

Sam[5]

---

4 At no point in the surviving letters docs Armando Castell make reference to the considerable amount of effort she was making to "break-into" the New York art scene. Though Thomas Boston remained a close friend to each, he seemed unable or unwilling to help her in career matters. In Armando Castell's journals, she notes that Boston snubbed her at art events several times and that he repeatedly "forgot" to introduce her to agents. Boston and Walldris were still in close communication at this time.

5 Here is another instance of a possibly destroyed or lost message, this one a package containing Walldris's photos. By this point he had stopped making sculptures altogether and was intent on documenting what he later termed "non-specific site-sculptures" both natural and man-made. Armando Castell's descriptions of the photos fit aesthetically with the few remaining from this time period in Walldris's estate, though there is no evidence he sent her similar images.

June 30, 1967:

Dear Jack,

If you think I'm asking you to come back, I'm not. I don't think it's a good idea. Stay with those trees. Stay with your "un-building." I like you more in the letters. I stitch you up and you listen to me speak/write for hours. Let me tell you about V because you asked me not to. She made this giant cock.[6] Well she didn't make it, she just bought it from that hidden sex shop across the street from the Portuguese bakery—the one that looks like it closed down a million years ago? She bought it and fucked it and now it's hers, that's how she "made" it. Jaja. Everyone had been sniffing around—then someone, it wasn't Thomas—he's never the first to do anything, though he usually gets the credit—someone gave it a lick. Then it was all anyone could do for a couple of nights was suck it and lick it and now V says, now that enough people have fucked it, it's not hers anymore, toodaloo and off to the races. Awful, huh? Nobody tried that with my wombs. Not that they would even know where to begin.

I know you don't want to hear about The Scene-Scene and I don't want to write about it, it's so stupid, but I'm reminding you of all you hate in the city because I DON'T want you coming home just now when I'm actually working and working and I can't feel the tips of my fingers they're so pricked with these needles (Yeah, you could suck them,

---

6 There are several artists that this pseudonym might refer to who later went on to create influential pieces of Cunt Art. There is the possibility, too, that Armando Castell is referring to one of her own pseudonyms. She never directly mentions her involvement with the Feminist Art Movement to Walldris, nor does she allude to her extensive correspondence with other women artists, namely Adrian Piper, who profoundly influenced her ideas on conceptual art.

make them soft again, make them good for anyplace and any type of skin). But I'm saying <u>don't come home, baby</u>, you never know what you may find. Who's in your bed, who's left (what in) it.[7]

On July 1, 1967, Jack Walldris wrote:

DEAR SAM,[8]

THERE'S TOO MUCH EXPLAINING TO DO. ARE YOU RICKY AND I'M LUCY?[9] I'M NOT GONNA DO IT. I'LL TELL YOU ABOUT CALIFORNIA. PETEY'S GOT A PLACE IN SANTANDER BAY. THE TREES HERE ARE SO BIG IT MAKES ART JUST STUPID. PETEY'S BUSY MAKING STUFF, BUT I JUST STAND AND LOOK UP AT THE TREES. I MEAN THE EIF-FEL TOWER, OUR OLD GOLLY GEE EMPIRE STATE, YEAH I GET WHY PEOPLE MAKE THOSE NOW BE-CAUSE ONCE YOU'VE SEEN A REDWOOD, YOU GOTTA TRY. TELL THOMAS TO SHUT THE FUCK UP AND STAY AWAY-IF-HE-KNOWS-WHAT'S-GOOD-FOR-HIM. WHAT A LUG. I MISS THAT HIDEOUS FACE ON HIM. I DON'T KNOW ABOUT V'S NEW THING BUT YOU'RE RIGHT. I DON'T REALLY WANT TO KNOW. I'M NOT INTO ANYTHING THAT CAN HAPPEN INSIDE RIGHT NOW, LIKE IN A GALLERY OR MUSEUM. IF YOU'RE GONNA WRITE, KEEP STUFF LIKE THAT OUT OF IT. I DON'T WANT TO

---

7 Unsigned.

8 This is the first extant letter from Walldris. His letters are typed, with one exception. At this point, he has been in California for eleven months.

9 See Armando Castell's essay, "Ai, Mami!" *Canto Tierra*, Vol. 7 (1992), on Latinx stereotypes and Latina artists in the mainstream art world.

HEAR ABOUT THE SCENE-SCENE. I'M GETTING
OVER IT. I'M DONE WITH THOSE BOXES. LET
THOMAS PAINT HIS NAME ON THEM. I'M NOT
MAKING ANYTHING FOR A WHILE. I'M CARVING
OUT ALL THE SHIT I'M NOT INTO. WHAT'S LEFT?
MAYBE NOTHING. THAT'D BE GREAT.

HERE'S A LIST OF GOOD THINGS I SAW TODAY:
TREES, REALLY TALL AND STRAIGHT, EVEN
THOUGH THEY'RE NOT QUITE STRAIGHT,
THEY'RE STRAIGHTER THAN YOU COULD HAVE
MADE UP.

THE BRIDGE IS GREAT. BETTER THAN OURS
EVEN. THE BRIDGE + THE FOG.

I SAW SOME MUD AND ROCKS I LIKE. THEY
GET BIGGER THE CLOSER YOU GET TO THEM. IS
THAT WHAT YOUR "WOMBS" ARE ABOUT?

THIS LIST IS CORNY.

XXOO, JACK

July 6, 1967:

DEAR SAM,

I DREAMED OF ALL THAT LAND BETWEEN
US. WELL IT WASN'T A DREAM, I WAS THINKING
OF YOU, WIDE AWAKE, THAT MORNING LOOK
YOU GET, DIRTY AS ANYTHING, YOU KNOW?
BUT THEN IT DID GET TO BE A DREAM BECAUSE
I GOT TO REALLY THINKING ABOUT ALL THAT
LAND BETWEEN US. HOW I WANTED TO REACH
ACROSS IT, HOW I WANTED YOU, BUT THAT LAND
WAS IN THE WAY, BUT MAYBE I WANTED THAT
LAND TOO. BIG MOUNTAINS RISING, FURRY

SCRUB BRUSH, THAT LONG, LONG, LONG CURVE
OF DESERT. AND I WAS ABOVE IT ALL, BIG, BUT
STILL NOT BIG ENOUGH, REACHING, BUT NOT
GETTING FAR ENOUGH. IS THAT A POEM OR A
DREAM OR AN ART PIECE, THOSE MOUNTAINS,
YOUR DIRT? STRETCH AND PRIME. MY MOUTH
IS FULL OF SALT AND PINE NEEDLES, BABY. WANT
YOU SO BAD.

JACK

July 14, 1967:

SAMMY, BABY, SWEETIE. COMING BACK TO
THE BIG OLE CRUNCH CRUNCH JONNY APPLESEED
NYC. ON THE BUS. SHOW UP IN THAT CROCHET
THING-Y. XXXXOOOOO[10]

---

10 No letters from Armando Castell during the late summer of 1967 remain. However, Walldris's brief return to New York City is well document-
ed. He held a "non-event" at The Jules-Clarke Gallery in the Lower East
Side on July 20, 1967, which was in large part possible due to Thomas
Boston's support and connections. The gallery rooms appeared completely
empty and after the first round of drinks, Walldris asked the guests to
leave because the "art had been ruined" by their presence. Boston refused
to heed Walldris (which may or may not have been Walldris's intentions)
and instead shot photos of the exhibit through the front windows. Boston's
photos of empty rooms in stark black and white contrasts are often used to
"document" Walldris's difficult to document "non-events" and "non-specific" work of the time. It is unclear whether Armando Castell was in
attendance, yet rumors quickly spread about the fight they had after the
event. In interviews she has given contradictory response on the question
of her attendance, her most recent being: "I don't know. It's hard to tell
with those things." (See: "A Life in Making: Collected Interviews with
Samantha Castell," *Art Forum*, May (2017): 23–54.)

Dated October 6, 1967, Walldris wrote the following letter by hand, presumably on the cross-country Greyhound.

Dear Sam,

On the bus through IOWAILLINOISINDIANAOHIO-PENNSYLVANIA NEWYORK and the ground is black earth furrows, rows and rows, from digging up the corn. Some of the stalks still left in the fields—starving ladies all twisted the same way. Remember riding this route with me when we were little babies, never seen the scene-scene, but wanting to more than ANYthing? That dirt's a painting, the best one I ever saw—your face reflected against the smudged bus window and the black earth behind it. Nobody could paint it, but I wonder what it would cost to try.

This is the part when I'm down on my knees begging to be forgiven—imagine 100 pages with just the word SORRY written over again and again. 100 pages you don't see. I shouldn't have done it, I'm an asshole, I'm an asshole.

But the bus I'm on is going the wrong way. It's the one I got on and I'm on it, no getting off. I wrote IOWAINDI-ANAOHIO, but I should have written OHIOINDIANAIOWA KANSAS NEBRASKA. NEVADA. Those states going west. The direction I'm heading. Back to CALIFORNIA. California. The dirt is the same either way you go. Only you can read this letter and I swear I got a poison on it that will shrivel those pretty fingers of yours so you'll never stitch again if you show this to anyone. You're bleeding all this out of me, baby. You are making me sticky-sweet. I took some photos when we stopped. Put your letters in the dirt and took a photo of that— one blew away—the ground was frozen and it crunched beneath my feet—those frost whiskers that make the same arch as the wheels that churned up the dirt. I wonder if I'll ever have enough dough to bring all this dirt into a gallery. I mean all of it. But I'd have to get your face too and that's impossible now. Nobody else's face would work. I want to call this dirt The Work—not what I've taken photos of or what I might one day be able to drag in, but the dirt as it is now, dead and ready to be churned up, the whole country, but mostly you.

You already know it all,

Jack

On **September 12, 1967**, Armando Castell wrote one of her last letters to Walldris:

Dear Jack,

I don't know that visuals are gonna work here. I don't think that mess between us last summer is something I can paint. I told you not to come back to New York.

V's got a tape recorder now. She's got amps and a guitar she just spits on. I wish I'd had her recorder that night. I'd have liked to be able to document what happened. But I don't know if I could—catch that kind of sound. How do you catch that? If you can't see it, you can't hear it? You see, I'm trying with my words, trying with this machine and dead tree pulp—not related to your Redwoods, I hope? If I'd had that recorder, I know what it would have sounded like. You'd be talking about California and I'm giggling, giggling like the dumb cunt that I am and you talk about the grant (that I helped you get) and how they want to give you more so you're going to start something out there. But then it all goes to feedback. I don't mean when you start yelling, I mean the feedback starts <u>with me</u>. My voice, telling you that you're not going and I'm not going, my voice that would say what I'm not allowed to you. That's what the machine can't record. Me neither. I can't record it and you, you couldn't even hear it. There would be just a wall of sound—not when you became your worst, but with my voice that would be blamed for starting it. That's not it. I pushed you, it's true and you slammed into the record player and you chased after me and I was screaming—again words that can't be preserved—and I stopped at the landing and I said, <u>you're not making anything and it's not fair that you get to say you're an artist even though you're not doing anything</u>, and you raised your fist at me and you stopped before it broke across my skin. You were so scared, more scared even than me, but there was a part of you that was like, so what, why shouldn't I be able to, if I want to?

There's no way I can keep my voice. No way anyone else can hear it. If I can't make you hear me, what's the point of these island-wombs? It's that my voice simply does not exist, and trying to make it creates a bomb of static and incoherence. Your exhibit was like nothing. And I know that's the point. You say no art, no artist. <u>Fine</u>, but I just became a person. You think it's not cool to make art you can see, or art about yourself—well, <u>my</u> self is barely real yet. I won't let anyone kill it, least of all you. What does this have to do with the wombs? I want to make something that's both mine and can actually be seen even though <u>I</u> made it. Something beyond a voice that can't be heard. The wombs are solid. They're everywhere you look.

You know there's no sending this,
Sam

Armando Castell did in fact send the above letter, though not until years later when she heard that Walldris was gravely ill with complications from Hepatitis C. They had both experienced financial and critical success by that time, though kept to their own respective coasts. Armando Castell's career, of course, would continue for several decades after Walldris's.

Addressed to his foundation in Marin County, Armando Castell's final package contained Walldris's letters to her, a single "womb-island-work" (probably one of her earliest), and the following letter:

November 1, 1987:

Jack,

Rather than say I miss you I'll say: Remember when we first met Thomas and he asked what our "introductory aesthetic experience" was and I pretended not to understand the question and mentioned some Picasso I'd seen when there was that exhibit in Houston when we were kids? He thought I was so boring, which was my point. I didn't like him even then. But you were so wanting to impress and I wanted to make fun of you for that. What did you say yours was? I can't remember. Something about music or the trains? I do know mine. I did then too, but I wanted to keep it secret. Now I'll tell you: Remember those dust devils that would happen outside of town? On the gravel roads that were just long stretches of dried grass on either side of them? Miniature tornadoes, wreaking havoc on the bits of gravel and dried leaves in their path? I remember when I saw my first one. A perfect whirl, but calm in the center, and I thought—I was 7 or something—I thought, I want to live in there. Not the metaphor of it, eye of the storm, destructive power with a calm center, well, that a little. But I loved the way it <u>looked</u>. A contained wildness and the rules about how things were supposed to move totally upset in such a gorgeous way. I wanted my whole life to be like that. Everything: my art, my clothes, my house, my body. A devastation of air on a plain. It makes its own world. I wanted in.

I'm sending you your letters, what's yours, still and strangely somehow,

Sam

Letters compiled and edited by Caridad Mirian Armando-Mendoza. Armando-Mendoza holds an MFA from The School of the Art Institute. She is an artist living in Chicago.

LOLI & MAGDA

When Loli called me up last night she drew my name out the way she used to when she wanted something from me. When she'd call to say she wasn't coming home, but wouldn't tell me where she was. Her lisp slight with most words, but stronger when she shaped my name. *Nathanael,* she'd say, the vowels catching in her mouth, tongue not quite clipping the Anglo *th,* so she sounded, unnervingly, like the women in my family who spoke only Spanish, though Loli grew up speaking English. I pictured her in a phone booth somewhere, though of course they're long gone, but still I see her: lips to the receiver, hand cupped around her mouth to block the wind, phone tight against her ear. *Nathanael. Can I ask you something?*

When she called last night, there was no wind batting her words. She didn't seem to want anything from me and I knew where she was. Her and her sister were making rabo— *get out of the city,* she said, *come up to see us.* It was the first time I'd heard her voice in months. I asked if I could bring her something, from her old pottery studio or the apartment, and she said, *No. Come just to see me.*

After we broke up, Loli moved to her sister's house on the lake in Wisconsin. We'd gone there together a couple of times—but only when her sister was out of town because she didn't like visitors. Magda was two years older than Loli.

Their grandparents on their mother's side had money, but they'd completely ignored Loli and Magda growing up. It was a big surprise when the grandparents died and, tucked in their will, was a college fund for Loli and the lake house for Magda. Magda was supposed to sell the house and use the money to pay for tuition once she finally decided on a place to go. She kept the house instead.

It took me an hour to get out of Chicago and then another two to get up to the lake. I didn't remember the drive being that long. No one goes out there in November. The clouds hung low and tattered and the waves stung even a hundred feet from the shore. The house, Magda's house, was one of those turn-of-the-century getaways, built back when they thought it was all space here. The property was laced with wooden walkways bleached white by the wind. Dune grass edged up through the planks. Loli had always hated the house. She said after a long weekend, just when we were leaving, *I've never felt like I'm allowed here.* Driving down the lane last night, I rolled the sentence around, considering the different meanings her words might have held for her. How *allowed* and *here* and even *I* could change and split in her mind, all she was saying in addition to what she said. Before she left, I'd asked her why she wanted to move somewhere no one was allowed to visit and she said that was why.

Somebody—Loli, because I'm sure Magda would never—had set up luminarias along the long driveway, the glowing brown paper bags propped almost waist-high on the crusted-over snow. I was glad for them—cloudy night, no moon. A state park lined both sides of the property, so there was no other light to help guide me. I turned off my headlamps for a second, to see how far I could go with just those flickering, crumpled shapes in the snow to guide me.

"Is your car broken again?" Loli asked before I was even

in the door.

I stood on the huge porch, holding my bottles of wine, unsure if I was really invited, if I'd made it up, unsure how or if I could touch her.

"I could see your headlights going on and off—it kinda spooked me."

She'd been watching then, perhaps her and Magda together, from the big front window, their eyes on me since I turned into the driveway. I'd thought I was alone—just me and the candles and the dark.

"Good thing I put up the fairy lights," she said.

She could have been on something. I could never tell, maybe it was nothing at all. She leaned into me and bumped her cheek against mine, kissing the air by my ear, once on both sides, like I was family.

"You know Magda, of course," she said.

I didn't really. I'd seen her at Loli's dad's family events—Noche Buena and the Armando Castell family reunions—but she'd never spoken to me and she didn't like visitors, or the city, or men, I assumed. Magda didn't lean in to kiss me, but nodded at her sister, turned around, and walked back into the house.

"I brought some wine," I said, holding up the bottles, like I needed proof of payment for my entrance.

"Well, Magda doesn't drink," Loli said. "But you know I love a little vino."

She weighed more than when I last saw her and her hair was long. She still had on the same old clothes, but they clung to her now as if they were covering a real human body and not just angles of elbows and ankles.

"I like your hair," I told her, wanting to touch it.

"I always said I was going to get fat." She rolled her eyes and shrugged. "At least I'm learning Spanish."

"How are you doing that?" I asked. I didn't mention the weight because I liked it and knew Loli didn't, was probably terrified of it. I didn't really care about my question either, just wanted to keep our words moving back and forth, to feel that pressure lifted and received.

"I've got a book," she said. "And I'm listening to this local public radio station. Today they had a spoken word piece called *Chicharrones Chokes Chirping Child* and this guy talking about government conspiracies—9/11 and the way the towers *actually* fell. Radio's mostly in English, though."

"Is that what you do all day up here?"

"No es un sombrero," she spoke in a purposefully-gringo accent, pointing to my hat. "Soy una mujer. Come on, Nate, it's too cold in the foyer."

The house was dark, lit only by gas lights, their copper wires curving through the high rafters, though regular electricity had been installed a decade ago. In the summer it was too hot to turn on the gas lights, but now I wanted to stay beneath the warm, hissing flames caught in miniature white nets. Loli opened and closed each door after we came through—"to keep the heat in," she kept saying. The doors all had old-fashioned latches and locks, the lock only on the outer side. The house felt like it was never empty, occupied by two people with not enough to fill their days, that not-enough so thick I could feel it as I passed through each room.

"We moved to the servant's quarters," Loli said. "It's warmer down here—the ceilings are lower and it's less creepy than having to go up two flights of dark stairs each night."

"It's creepier upstairs?"

"You betcha." She sounded like her mom then and I couldn't tell if she was joking or serious. I imagined a life where you brought your servants to your summer home and had wings for them to stay in—and to stay out of sight. Where I'd be in this world, where Loli would be. The kitchen was reachable through a small sunroom, both later additions, and by the time we got there, I was so turned around I worried I couldn't find my way out alone.

In the kitchen, Loli turned towards me beneath one of the pools of light and held my gaze.

"You know I can't cook, but I made the salad," she said.

I knew she could cook very well. She used to blaze through cookbooks and had several magazine subscriptions whose recipes she cut out and ranked. When I said nothing, she spoke again.

"Magda makes the best rabo in the family."

"Sounds great."

Magda was fiddling under the sink and she still hadn't looked our way. I was beginning to feel like she didn't know I was coming until I showed up. The air felt thin from the lamps and the wood stove sucking oxygen. But I wondered too if everything Loli was saying was a lie, if this was one of her games, and my job was to catch her at it, to know that the opposite of what she said was true, to do the opposite of what she told me.

"I'm really glad to be here," I said to Magda. "I haven't left Chicago in months."

She turned to me finally and squinted as if I'd just said something really racist or in Finnish. Then she stuck her head back under the sink.

The table was round and Loli was careful to sit directly across from me. Magda settled in on her left side without a word. I kept moving my chair, trying to get closer to Loli, but she was always ahead of me.

Magda, who "didn't drink," finished the wine I brought and set a big plastic bottle of Korbel on the table midway through dinner. She kept pouring brandy, breaking ice from ancient metal molds into our glasses and getting up to add logs to the fire. By the time dinner was over, I was sweating and Loli's face was blotched with red. The windows of the kitchen had fogged, but Magda just kept adding logs, staying in front of the fire until tiny beads of sweat appeared on her forehead. When she stared into the stove, her face relaxed and she looked just like Loli.

After we'd eaten all the rabo—the oxtail hadn't been cooked long enough and was still chewy, meat stuck to the bone—Loli picked at the burnt bits of beef and onions on the side of the pan, flipping them into her mouth like rough, dark stones. She crunched the slices of garlic at the bottom of the salad bowl and then picked up our plates. Magda sat staring at the fire—the door of the stove open and kicking heat.

"Remember that sculpture you made in freshman year," I said. "That ox with, like, eight tails?"

"No," Loli said.

"Yeah, you do—it was supposed to be a joke. Like how that would be every Cuban's dream, an ox with all these extra tails to make rabo."

Magda snickered. "Who would even get that joke? At *your* school?"

"But the tails kept falling off in the kiln—remember? You spent days on it."

"I'm too hot to remember," Loli said.

She leaned over the sink to press her cheek to the window, leaving a heart shape that quickly frosted over. She wrote something in the frost I couldn't read and wiped it away, then brought that hand to her face, to the back of her neck.

Magda grabbed more wood from the hall and put it in the stove.

"Come on, Maggi," Loli said. "It's already too much in here."

"I have to keep this fire going," Magda said. "Or else you'll complain all night."

Magda's face was blotched red too, her black curls falling over her eyes, baby hairs sticking to her cheeks and making their way to the corners of her mouth.

I thought about the drive home, the wine, the heat. I thought about asking Loli if I could stay, about why she'd brought me up here.

"El fuego es un fuente," Loli pointed at the stove, doing her exaggerated telenovela accent that always made me laugh and made her lisp sound Castilian. "Una mesa limpia da la gloria," she said, tapping the dirty table. "Whoever built this house probably thought nothing like that would ever be said here. And now I'm saying it."

"The point of which is still unclear," Magda said.

Loli turned even redder, but didn't respond. Magda closed the wood-stove door, then opened it again slowly for a draft.

"We do get out, you know," Loli said, suddenly. "I even dragged Magda to the outlet mall last weekend."

"It was a shit show," Magda said, pouring more Korbel. "White suburban moms. Not even soccer moms, like, too rich for their kids to play soccer."

"Yeah—*lacrosse* moms," Loli said. "But you got into it. You were fighting in the sale bins for the lace thongs."

"Yeah, right," Magda said and for the first time she looked right at me. I looked at the black, frosted windows.

"We both got great bathing suits," Loli said. "They were on sale because it's winter. They're really cute and designer brands. Pretty good for the boonies."

She was looking right at me too, but more closed off. What was she doing in this house? Hours from a decent kiln? Hair unflicked by glaze, clothes clean, body twitching and hovering, so unlike when she was working, wearing the same filthy coveralls for days: exhausted, but solid.

"You should put them on," I said. "The swimsuits." I don't know how I said it and I looked away when I did.

"Okay," Magda said and walked out of the room. Loli laughed like Magda was bluffing, but stopped when her sister didn't come back.

"Yeah, okay, it'll be fun," Loli got up and followed Magda.

That left me alone in the kitchen, the loud pops of sap in the stove breaking up the rush of words in my head. I tried to start the dishes, but I didn't know how to turn on the hot water. The water from the faucet was freezing. I poured myself more brandy and checked the fridge for some pop.

They'd left the door to the sunroom open, but I could feel them come into the kitchen on the back of my neck. The air shifted—my body some kind of barometer. I didn't know how to turn around.

"Ta da!" Loli threw her arms in the air and twirled around. Their suits were matching lime green bikinis with plastic gold rings at their sternums and hips. The gold rings pushed against Magda's pelvic bones, the triangles of her bikini cupped against bony ribs. But Loli's skin pressed back at her suit, forcing the gold rings to dig into the soft spaces at her hips. This deep in winter, the skin on their shins and upper arms was dull and dry. It was as if they had switched bodies. Magda rolled her eyes at my staring and went to the fire.

"Stoke it up, Magda!" Loli said, twirling again. "Well, what do you think?"

"They're good," I said. "More South Beach than Lake Michigan, but they look good."

"I know it's corny to have matching ones, but they were both on sale."

Darkness on the Edge of Town had been looping for a while. Loli went to change it, sashaying the whole time I was sure. She brought her record player to the lake house along with all her warped records in their moldy sleeves. I couldn't really look at her. I was happy and I didn't want her to see. She put on something I didn't recognize, a woman singing slowly with an accent I couldn't place. A fado maybe, or its Brazilian equivalent.

"Come on, Magda," Loli said. "Even in my suit I'm sweating." She grabbed a checkered napkin and wiped her face with it, reached again to the icy window and smeared her hand on her bare stomach. When Magda didn't react, Loli crept up behind her and put her cold, wet hand on her back. I could see the ripple roll down Magda's skin like she was made of dune sand, but she didn't turn. Loli leaned close to her ear and whispered something I couldn't hear. Magda shook her head. Loli leaned in again, pouted, then walked over to me. I still couldn't look at her.

"You want something else?" she asked me, and I shook my head. She tried to get more meat off the pan, but it was covered in soap bubbles. "Magda, please," she said and slammed the pan down into the dirty water. "Just dance with me for one song. For half a song."

Magda closed the stove door, set down her glass and walked over to Loli. She grabbed Loli's hips and moved them back and forth to the music, but with too much force and too quickly, like she was trying to break something instead of dance. Loli stepped forward and put her arms around her sister's neck. They moved towards the stove, Loli leading and keeping them clear of the hot iron. They slowly circled the table in their lime green bikinis, their faces red like flushed saints. When they came by me, their bare legs brushed against mine, but they kept moving like they didn't notice, swaying slowly, slightly offbeat, around the room.

We smoked, Loli found more brandy, we squished onto an ancient loveseat in the corner and watched Carmen Castell films on a projector Madga rigged up. I knew almost every shot, I'd seen them so many times with Loli, but they seemed different somehow, maybe it was the location, maybe it was the time of night. Then, late, real late, Loli and Magda started dancing again and I tried to dance with them. The brandy was gone and soon it would be light. I stood up and Magda dropped her hands from Loli's hips. Loli and I circled the table once, slow and awkward.

"Nathanael," she said.

"Ask me anything."

But she was silent. Wouldn't speak, not a lie or a question—nothing. I cupped her chin in my hand and tried to kiss her. She pushed me back into my chair at the table. I was so surprised by what I'd done that she really was able to push me and I sat there, like I couldn't get back up.

Magda stayed crouched down in front of the fire facing away from me. Loli grabbed an old rug from the sunroom and draped it around her and Magda's shoulders. The rug was filthy—sand and dirt dropped off it when Loli picked it up, landing in a hiss on the floor. Where their bare knees and ankles poked out from under the rug, their skin was daubed in dust and the short hair of a long-dead pet. Loli spoke just above a whisper, cheek pressed against Magda's, all words I knew, but none I could hear. Magda leaned against Loli's ear, her lips almost grazing the lobe when she turned.

I tried to kiss Loli again and she told me to stop and I guess I didn't. I think Magda got between me and Loli and pulled Loli away from me. They must have moved quickly around the kitchen table and then shut the door to the sunroom behind them, locking me in, locking me out.

When I woke up the fire was cold and I was alone on the floor, leaning against the door to the sunroom, the impression of the wood on my forearm and cheek. I woke because the lock on the other side had clicked and the door had eased open. At first, I thought one of them had opened it, but was just the old latch giving way. Through the thud and haze of sleep, the latch opening was what woke me, that tiny sigh, and I told myself later I was waiting for that sound because with that door locked, I couldn't leave, I'd be stuck in their kitchen forever.

In the sunroom, they had pulled sofa cushions and blankets to the floor. They were still sleeping, curled around each other, like a single lithe sea creature, many-limbed and sloping along the ocean floor. I tried to push myself to my feet, but it was too hard and they were only a body's length away, reachable easily on my knees. A concentrated beam of sunlight traveled through the thick, rippled glass and hit their bare shoulders. Soon the light would make its way to their faces, waking them. I brushed the hair off their foreheads, trying not to touch their skin. Where I failed, it felt like my fingertips were burning. I opened my mouth. I knew just what I wanted to whisper into Loli's ear, that well of quiet. But I couldn't speak a word.

MR. A AND COMPANY

The performance:
Mr. A speaks: "First there is the white."

We stop mid-dance and grab the tubs of white grease paint balanced on the rock face. We cradle our tools—makeup, cosmetic sponge—in our hands, waiting to become dead bodies on this mountain ledge. To dance as dead.

"But first there is the removal," he says.

We sigh. The removal. Just because Mr. A is accustomed to the frozen winds of northern Japan, he thinks the rest of his dance troupe is too. Some of us are not, some of us were raised on a gentle Caribbean isle, where we were never cold (though often hungry), and only saw snow on old Soviet educational films. But this is negative-pattern thinking: a sign of non-commitment and refusal to fully kill the body.

"The removal of the layers," Mr. A says. "The layers of cloth, the layers of self. To dance as dead."

My former lover is giving me absolutely alive eyes from across the precariously-balanced bamboo stage. He is preventing the death of my body.

"Pick up the cloth," Mr. A says.

We all reach for our jackets and sweatpants, hoping we can put them back on. The wind is terrible on this mountain.

"The white cloth," Mr. A corrects us.

Coño.

"The white cloth, the small one," he says. "A triangle of white and knotted cloth."

He means our loincloths, though they're more like g-strings, as in the final item a stripper peels off, not the only thing to wear on a frozen mountain. The loincloth is also my former lover's preferred attire regardless of the weather, if he must wear anything at all.

Mr. A jabs one of his bony fingers in between my ribs. His fingers say, die the body, rise the dead voice. Ow.

Before the performance:

But before we could undress and dress according to Mr. A's instructions, we had to wait for him to recover. Mr. A is a master dancer, though he would never use that word. His most recent solo show, "The Dance of the Dead Sea"— performed last month in downtown Osaka and to much acclaim—had left him ragged. His seventy-something-year-old body does not limit his dance, but it does require rest. After his dance, Mr. A said the salt of the Dead Sea had stayed in his body. His stomach was a cave of salt formations. We waited for three days on this mountain ridge, nestled next to stone, hiding from the wind. For Mr. A to become less heavy and less tired. For him to teach our bodies to move like his.

Mr. A chose this specific ridge by the sea due to the smooth ledge it provides for dancing and the tiered ridge directly below for the audience members. Decades ago, his own teacher danced the tale of Ama the Lady Diver here, which we will be performing tonight. The ridge is surrounded by steep cliffs, dusted by white snow and slick ice, all prominent elements in Mr. A's aesthetics. The performance will begin in less than four hours, but remains unchoreographed. In the second to last group performance, the rope suspending the dancers high in the air broke and one dancer was not revived. The audience doesn't know what to expect from this performance, but they will be expecting something.

Retrieval of Personal History:

Once, I lived a caged life. After I defected from my island (my ballet troupe had been given special permission to perform in Toronto and each of us took that special opportunity to disappear into the freezing city), I was eventually granted amnesty in Berlin. At the time, I wanted never to see my island again. I knew that by leaving in the way I did, I could never return. In Berlin, my movement studies centered around leaving the body. Around exerting my will on the body. Around bringing the body into the air when all it wants is to howl from the earth's core. My practice then was lifting. Lifting my body, powered by ego, off the ground and into the sky. I was involved in numerous unhealthy relationships that imitated and exacerbated this desire, and one of the men with whom I was involved followed me here, ostensibly to be a part of Mr. A's Dance Company. One might more accurately say he has followed me everywhere: on the island, when we were children jittery from our sugar-water dinner, scrambling up the sea wall; to the stage in Toronto; to here, the mountain's edge. More second self than the other names I have called him. My former lover said he is here only to dance, but I don't believe him.

Before the performance:

As a warm-up exercise and to express my independence from my former lover, I decided to throw myself repeatedly against the rock face and then fall in the crucifix pose backwards onto the bamboo stage. No one else in the troupe can do the fall. My former lover's own attempts at the crucifix fall have resulted in either breaks of form or bone.

I spread my arms, arched my neck, and fell backwards, body straight, *extremely* slowly. I landed without the use of my hands or bending my back. It took an entire minute. My former lover watched me fall.

Tale of Ama the Lady Diver: Ama lived by the ocean, where she fished for clams and pearls. She dove beneath the freezing waves wearing only a loincloth and carrying only a machete. She tied a long white rope to a rock on the surface and used the rope to descend and ascend from the water. The rope her only path up from the depths.

Ama had a dear little son and one day, the ocean took her son for its own. She would not allow this to be. She knew how worlds could divide. Land and water. Water and sky. She knew that at the point of the divide was an opening. She knew there she would find her son.

Retrieval of Personal History:

When I was very young, my mother would make a dish she called simply *hervido*. She said it was an old Armando Castell family recipe, but the open name, which described only its method of cooking, allowed her to put anything she wanted or could finagle from the ration line in it. Whatever she put in the pot—bits of dried fat, pig ears, yuca, beans—was always cheap and sometimes filling. But the secret reason for making this dish—as thrift at the cost of sensual pleasure was both emblem and necessity of the revolution—was that the dish contained so much water she could leave it on the stove, perform fellatio on the downstairs neighbor, and return without fear of supper being burnt. I am exaggerating slightly about the fellatio. I only saw her doing that to the downstairs neighbor twice. Mostly, she liked to leave the dish on the stove in order to lie on the bathroom floor. I liked to lie with her, straining to hear the ocean, counting tiles, and imagining what we would do to the spiders on the ceiling if we had the bravado and mercilessness to trap them. One evening, she neither fellated nor lay on the bathroom floor. In fact, she managed not to overcook the dish, even added fresh cilantro she grew on the windowsill in an old vegetable oil tub. My father—once engineer, now busboy—fresh from some fellating of his own, greeted my mother warmly and sat down to dinner. Theirs was a mad, passionate love. Instead of serving the meal, my mother waited—shooing us away or giving out small tasks in the kitchen to keep us busy. When the dish had mostly cooled, she upturned the entire pot on her head. Our family mutt, Rambo, delighted at not having to work to earn this extra food, licked fervently at my mother's calves where bits of onions and gizzards were stuck. My father, in utter adoration and supplication, began to do the same, starting with the yuca on the cracked linoleum floor and working his way up. My mother had fought to get the pot's contents, but she needed to overturn the pot, she needed the arch of her arms above her head, the bowing and slurping. She needed an act of total immersion and folly. That was the moment I knew I was a dancer.

Tale of Ama the Lady Diver: To save her son, Ama dropped her white rope into the water and waited until it had sunk to the bottom of the deepest ocean well. She dove into the sea, following the rope, and finally reached the palace of the dead. There she found the great jewel. The jewel that would save her son. She made a cut underneath her breast and tucked the jewel into the wound. She began the climb up towards the surface. The line of her blood from beneath her breast ran parallel to the white rope bringing her to air. She was dead when she broke from the water.

Before the performance:

The choice of Ama the Lady Diver is a strange one for Mr. A. Throughout his career, he has rejected the maternal, focusing instead on playing aging gigolos, suicidal lovers, relics of explosive atoms. We know nothing of his family life. On the mountain cliff, we contemplated this anomaly, Mr. A's sudden turn towards the origin of all.

Western scholars consider Ama an Orpheus figure, or the un-Orpheus. Returning with what she sought, but returning dead. I recognized the story of Ama the Lady Diver the first time I heard it. I grew up on tales of women rising out of the ocean.

The performance:

After days of waiting, something goes through us—a taut plait—and we know Mr. A is waking. Soon he will rise. Killing the body is our practice. With the dead body we dance. We ready our tubs of white makeup and sponges. With them we will become dead. As dead as he is.

We will begin the performance wrapped in cloth woven in part with hair—our own, our beloved pets. We will be woven into the hair and through the course of the performance strips of cloth will be cast off the mountain cliffs as a preliminary offering to the dead. We are unsure what happens next. We understand that this is how Mr. A creates. My former lover has made a bed of the excess cloth in a corner of the mountain ridge, but I refuse to lie in it. The nest of hair he wove is similar to our old bed in Berlin. That bed contained many limbs and many pasts, woven around themselves. This nest contains many strands, all knotted together.

It is now clear that the specks on the rocks below are not snow monkeys bathing in hot springs, but audience members beginning the laborious climb towards us. A certain desperation enters our expressions. My former lover, streaked in white paint, undulates before me. I contemplate another crucifix fall. Mr. A turns his head slightly and looks at me with a funny smile. I have told Mr. A my tale of the boiled dinner and the mutt Rambo and my father on his knees. He knows this is the one personal memory I cannot commit to dance. It is my wish: to kill the body enough that I may play all the roles—my mother, my father, Rambo, the yuca and the wilted cilantro.

Mr. A rises. He tells us to dress in only our loincloths. To paint our bodies white. Mr. A speaks: "The dead body is white. The outline of ash. A body thrown against a wall by molecules. The color left behind by bone."

We listen to Mr. A.

"Silence the I," he says. "Forget the self with the white paint. My mother—"

We stop moving and listen. Mr. A has never spoken of his mother.

"My mother," he says again. He looks down at the audience member specks moving closer.

"My—" he stammers.

"Now the white paint," he continues, his voice steady again. "White eyes white mouth. All white now."

My former lover is still watching me. I have difficulty looking away.

Retrieval of Personal History:

The second to last group performance took place on top of the Chase Equity building in downtown Osaka at 7:00 a.m. I was not a member of the troupe at the time. I have been told that the training for that performance was excruciating, but it resulted in the most dead-like bodies on stage in the history of the dance company. The troupe, dressed in business suits, jumped repeatedly from the roof of the building and unfurled long red streamers as they fell. Before they touched the ground, invisible ropes around their abdomens held tight and caught them. It did not catch all of them. I— for I was *I* then—was shamed by my reluctance to help. The coldness I felt seeing their—for they were *they* then—fall.

Tale of Ama the Lady Diver: Ama's son lived and grew, but he did not know his home or his mother. He did not know a jewel was brought from the palace of the dead beneath the sea to save him. He did not know of his mother's blood, slipping out into salt water, one hand clasped to the jewel hidden under her breast.

The performance:

Now we are unfurling the same red streamers as in the Chase Equity performance. They are the same and yet not the same because their purpose will be different. Tonight, they are tongues. We have attached them to thick hemp rope, like stockings on a laundry line. We will stand behind them, eyes rolled into the back of our heads, bow-legged and hunched over like poor farmers. Mr. A dances among us, catching some, letting others fall. My former lover dances close to me. I told him not to join the troupe. Neither my desire nor amity towards him has ceased, but if I wish to dance the dance of death, I must cut all ties to my island of life. Only then might I be reborn as each of my memories, separately contained within one body, no room for longing left. My former lover drops to his knees. His tongue slowly circles the space around my toes. My former lover is reenacting the scene of the spilled dinner. He is my father kneeling, my mother dripping broth. He plays all the roles I know, and another. I can feel the heat of his body in stark contrast to the mountain wind. A body I know so well.

Retrieval of Personal History:

Once, getting off a train outside of La Habana, I saw a little boy calling for his mother. He had many suitcases around him and seemed unable to leave them. Perhaps they were tied to his body in an intricate series of leashes; memory is faulty. I looked around for the boy's mother and saw her walking away from him, allowing herself to be carried by the crowd towards the sea. He was wearing the bright, little shorts popular for children at that time and polished patent leather shoes. His hair had been recently cut. He kept calling her name, but she did not pause. She was walking very fast. With the care so natural among the very young, he opened the suitcases and arrayed the contents at the edge of the platform. Then he pushed them, one by one, onto the train tracks. Still his mother did not look back.

The performance:

Mr. A is smiling. When he smiles, he is a small child who has swallowed his mother, his father, and their family home. He is chewing through the copper pipes and cotton batting of an entire life. He does not intend to spit it out. Mr. A is telling us the tale of Ama the Lady Diver and—though we know it so well—when filtered through the ceramic hot pots, sliding doors, and pelvic bones of his smile, it becomes a place we can open and live in. Our bodies, now dead, can become the woman diving to the sea, her wounded breast punching from water. Her son bringing her there, but not back.

Tale of Ama the Lady Diver: Dead, but returning with the jewel, Ama saves her child. Years later, her ghost speaks to the grown son and he calls her a Holy One. She turns into a dragon and dances with joy. This is usually the end of the tale.

The performance:

Lady Ama dove into the sea to retrieve the jewel, but Mr. A does not know why.

"Why, Mother?" he asks.

To save her son, we answer with our bodies.

"But how can a jewel save a son?" my former lover asks this with his own voice. I move to dance, but realize I do not know the answer.

"Ama, Ama," the sound rolls out of Mr. A's mouth. This rolling becomes another sound. *Ama ama ama.* We are her, many-bodied, many-eyed, looking back and speaking as a body of what we see. The red tongues, now coming from our breasts, we are all lady divers and the mountain's rocks are the sea because in the mountain there is the sea, and in the sea, there is the mountain. We hide the jewel beneath our breasts and we resurface. Hide, resurface. We act as one rope guiding us all back to the light above the water. Weave the hair around our bodies. The hair is water, the hair is death, braiding into each other and out. Repeat the movements to Mr. A's words until each movement is engrained in our flesh like the ice breaking the mountain. We were born knowing this dance. We were dead knowing this dance. Mr. A touches one of our backs and we all crumble at the weight. Mr. A cries and we are inconsolable. Mr. A stops moving, stops talking, and we freeze. We know that to be as still as he is is to be very, very empty.

The audience gathers close. We hear them through our skin and smell their scent of shampoo and gasoline. We feel them settle around us, attentive and shivering. In our dance, we climb through the rock, swim through the rock that is now water, unleash the red streamers, cast off the woven hair.

But something in me still hears the question of my former lover. And still hears the voice that spoke it, dead as I want to be.

How can a jewel save anyone? No son asks for a jewel.

We reach the moment for Mr. A's solo. But Mr. A is not moving. He is not in the rehearsed location on the edge of the stage. Our bodies are trained to adapt, so we adapt. But he is not moving. He is supposed to be the jewel that comes out of us, but he is not jewel-like. His dead body barely flutters. He is so tired. Beneath the fluttering is a sound, the sound is *ama ama ama*. We stand still, some of us move and dive and swim, repeating the earlier motions. There is a strangeness coming from him that the audience is beginning to notice. All he says is *ama ama*. My former lover moves towards me slowly. He is dancing a new dance. He is a flash of gravel—not a careless barrage scattered by a passing tire, but a single stone picked up by a boy in short pants and tossed at shutters painted lime then coral then teal, their corners flaking and rotting in the salty air. He is dancing the sound I was missing from the dinner scene, among the lapping and overturning, the cilantro, Rambo, and my mother's heels. A stone tossed at my window asking me to play. The troupe moves around us. I do not attempt the crucifix fall. The troupe moves between us. Our bodies dance. They kneel and lap up broth that tastes like earth and meat. Our bodies are white ropes, blood slipping in water. I know I will return to my island.

"I left her," Mr. A says with his voice and his body. "I left her when they told me to and I did not look back and I do not know what they did to her."

I walk towards Mr. A. I kneel down and clasp his hand. I am moving him slowly through many layers of rock and cold water. He is rising. Alive and cored.

"Mother," he says.

"I'm here," I say, dancing towards him. "Let me hold you, my darling child."

THE FIELD OF PROFESSIONAL MOURNING

I try to judge from the preliminary phone conversation whether my client will require the full-length interview or the questionnaire. The first question I ask tells me a great deal: How did you hear about our services? We have internet ads generated by certain search-words: *death, passing, loss, survive.* We advertise in the online and print versions of the local papers, those that are still left. We have pamphlets in the visiting areas of local nursing homes and I am familiar with the clergy who work there.

The clients who have heard of our services from an online source are usually more comfortable with the questionnaire. They are used to conducting all sorts of personal business impersonally—staying just on this side of estrangement with family members. If they learned about my company from a pamphlet, a newsprint ad, or a clergy member, they are often more comfortable with a personal interview. But I have learned not to make assumptions. Some elderly, conservative clients wish to fill out a questionnaire. Some young people with high-end technical jobs want only to speak to a person.

The purpose of these questions is not their answers, but to gauge the client's level of grief—or more accurately, their relationship to their grief. My final question is usually already answered in the pauses, the unasked-for details, wavering or solidity of voice, the way they address me—Ma'am, Ms.

Castell, even, Sasha. But in my first phone conversation I always ask it, because of its importance: why have you decided to contact a professional mourner?

I started Castell and Friends two decades ago, right after college, and my business has been unrivaled for years. But a few months ago when my employees first stopped returning my calls, I had a horrible fear that one of them was trying to set up their own business with my clients and my employees. A poacher. I'd lost five employees in a month—more than I had in several years. It was the only explanation I could think of. There are no contractual obligations that prevent employees from forming their own business. My company is based on trust. I do not believe that what we do is lying. Rather, we experience true emotions: emotions channeled through our bodies, not generated by our minds. I found it awful to even consider deceit among my employees, all of whom I held in deep respect. But I did consider it and considered it of my favorite, Mónica.

The first question I ask all my potential employees during the interview process is: What draws you to the field of professional mourning?
   a) a desire to connect with people in pain
   b) a lack of feeling of connection to other people
   c) inability to grieve in the past
   d) need to express personal pain
   e) family tradition of professional mourners
   f) none of the above
   g) I don't know
   I only progress potentials to the next round if they answer e, f, or g. To the first question in the interview Mónica gave her own answer:

h) all of the above.

She came from a long line of professional mourners—Korean and Mexican. Mónica was covered in tattoos: sailors, hearts with cursive names, fairies, an elaborate cross encircled by a green serpent and roses, which I only saw much later. She walked like she'd just parted the seas herself, and she had long, thick hair that she never tied back.

Despite her unorthodox interview, her grief was so authentic that she became my top employee. In a way, Mónica had been training for years. Both her parents had taken her to services since she was a child. Her keen, coming from that huge torso, was fully developed, though she was only in her twenties. It began deep inside of her, high-pitched and vibrating throughout her bones, like a host of sparrows waking and realizing their roost is on fire. It would grow in sound and lower in pitch until it had depth—water rushing at you from deep inside a cave. But the most impressive part was the pauses. Instead of letting the keen die down slowly as her lungs were depleted of air, she stopped the sound abruptly at its crescendo. The silence between the last sound and the next existed in a way that few people do their entire lives. She answered all the interview questions wrong, but when I asked her to keen, I made my decision. Perhaps I should have been more careful.

<u>Client Questionnaire:</u>

Please answer all questions. Do not leave any blank. Feel free to inscribe additional remarks.

1) What role would you like your professional mourner (P.M.) to play in the service?

    a) mourner
    b) leader of service

    c)   keener (traditional mourning wail):
         i. specify tradition:
    d)   reader of elegy (elegy must be written previously by client)
    e)   other (please specify):

*Kindly note that our services are finalized at the end of the funeral/ memorial service. We do not under any circumstances extend our service beyond the structured meeting of personal mourners.

Several weeks ago, I received a disturbing call from a client about Mónica, and this, coupled with my fears about the loss of employees, made me decide I had to go see her after hours. Mónica had begun taking on more cases than I recommended. But because of the drop in employees, it was difficult for me to insist that she not attend services. Even before, she had been training multiple potential employees at once and offering informal counseling sessions to my other employees. Many of them had considered her my protégé, and though I showed no outward sign, I believed it too.

There had been several services where she was one of the only mourners in attendance. That week alone she attended three traditional wakes where she keened all night, refusing refreshment. It was from a client at one of these wakes that I received the call. He told me that Mónica had not left the personal mourners after the service ended, but had joined them in their homes and helped cook for the widower. The client, the grown son of the deceased woman, had not been complaining about Mónica's behavior, rather praising it. He said that he had been to many services with P.M.s and none of them had shown that level of concern for the entire family.

The word that frightened me: *concern*. A display distinct from professional grief. It was the most dangerous aspect of our job; that we would continue to feel for our clients after the service, that this would motivate behavior that further linked us to their lives. This behavior was always destructive, no matter the motives behind it.

Even though it was Mónica's day off, I got on the Red Line and headed towards her apartment. At that moment, I envisioned myself a bit of a detective: one of those old-fashioned, hard-boiled types I like to stay up all night reading about. If my suspicions were wrong, I could comfort her, play the experienced mentor, a role I liked.

The subway was damp and cool, though everyone on it was sweating, legs sticking to the blue plastic seats if you were lucky enough to grab one. At the stations downtown we stopped in front of ads for a new exhibit at the Art Institute: a black and white photo of a woman facing the camera, her palms open and outstretched, holding a thick braid. She's staring at you and her own hair is disheveled, raw, as if only moments ago she'd cut the braid she holds off her head. She was a filmmaker, I guess, or she filmed her performance art—one of those people you could never quite pin down just what it is they've done. She'd disappeared before she got famous, but a trove of her films and photos was found in rural Cuba, decades later, miraculously preserved. When the ads for her retrospective first went up, Mónica had asked if I was related to her—same last name, same tiny island—but I told her, honestly, I didn't know.

The train cut smoothly through the Loop, but stuttered to a stop in an unlit tunnel just north of State. We paused in the darkness, everyone tense. I hate it when the train stops in the dark. I know it's irrational, but I feel, each time, like I've been blotted out, like I've simply ceased to exist. Regardless of the suspicions I held about my business, I knew Mónica was engaged in something that made the muscles in my legs coil. Something that wouldn't let them relax even when we rose above ground and back onto the sun-drenched elevated track.

The city shrank as we headed north, buildings dripping light in the summer haze. Mónica lived in a tiny studio, far from the lake. One of those places that only exist in the mind because they are in a constant state of transition. They cannot be called neighborhoods anymore, but processes, places that mark movement from one condition to the next. Mónica's block looked decrepit, trash and diapers stuffed into large cracks in the sidewalk, fake brick siding peeling off of gutted homes. But the expensive strollers and small dogs pointed towards the falsity of the buildings' outward stasis. At this point, the buildings' nature was change, disappearance.

Sweating from the heat of the subway and the asphalt, I thought about my oldest employee. It used to be people only resigned from Castell and Friends after years of work, so it felt like it wasn't resigning, but closer to retiring. Ceely Armando had stayed with me after a move into assisted living, though she had gone down to only one service every couple of weeks. She'd grown up in Chicago, called streets by names even I'd never heard of, and had lived for decades in an apartment next to the Montrose Brown line stop with a white woman she still referred to as her "friend." She was so well-known, clients would often postpone a service just to ensure she could be there.

But I hardly noticed when she didn't call me back one week regarding booking a service.

I suppose this makes a certain sense. My work prizes people who can drift in and out of sight, swirl unseen beneath the surface of an interaction until their moment comes. I hire people who aren't interested in self, who are difficult to see, until the sight of them is necessary. Even then it is not them that is visible, but their grief.

After Ceely, though, people really started disappearing. Reliable employees did not return phone calls, left their apartments empty, cut off all contact with everyone they knew.

3) What level of grief would you like your P.M. to express?

   a) controlled & somber
   b) evidence of weeping though respectfully positive
   c) mild weeping
   d) moderate weeping
   e) heavy weeping
   f) controlled anger at deceased / guests (circle one or both)
   g) hysteria*

*For an additional fee, your P.M. can behave in a manner that will require their removal from the services, so great is their show of grief.

Mónica was in the middle of cooking something when she let me into her apartment. Steam rose from a pot on the stove, the grayed floral wallpaper above it crinkled and moist. Mónica had the sort of sweat one gets from staying inside too long. A layer caked along the seams of her shirt, the dew on her upper lips the same as what appears on zucchini when it just starts to sizzle. To steady myself from the climb up the stairs, I touched the wall, and parts of it—years of cooking and sweating—let go and rested on my palm. Asking Mónica if she was setting up her own professional mourning service with my employees outright would be impossible, but I didn't know any other way. I put down the bottle of mineral water and the dollar limes I had brought her from the bodega on the corner. Neither of us drink.

"Are you worried, Sasha?" she asked me, turning away from the stove, looking right at me, not faced away or fiddling with the limes like I would have. I wanted her to touch me. I realized then I'd wanted that since I first saw her.

"About what?" I said, reaching for the bag of the limes.

"About Castell and Friends. We're losing so many employees."

A detective would have taken her *we* to signify that she wasn't contemplating betrayal. Or maybe would have used the question itself to prove that she was. She moved closer to me and put her hand, oddly cold, on my arm, my upper arm, where bosses are not allowed to touch their employees. Forearms are allowed, but the nature of the touch is still important.

"Why do you think it's happening?" I asked. I knew my voice was barely audible. I could not look at her because then I would forget why I had come.

"I don't know, Sash. I really don't."

"You know," I said, moving away from her. "I've been worried that someone is trying to start a new business. A poacher. Have you heard anything?"

"No one would dare do that," Mónica said. "We all love you. Besides, how could they? They'd be shunned by the entire community. Castell and Friends is an empire."

Of course, I believed her. She looked right at me when she spoke. But the pesky detective in me thought, that is just what she would say if she was planning a move. And I remembered what she'd once said to me about how much she hated empires.

"The rice is ready," Mónica said. "You want some? Or are you going to eat alone at Maharaja's again?"

I looked up. "How do you know?"

"I walk by you in there most nights. I never have the guts to come in."

Standing in front of the mirror in her bedroom, Mónica began unbuttoning my dress. The drape was down halfway against the almost-gone sun. Her arms orange where the light hit and most of her in shadow. She kept her eyes on mine, so she didn't see what she was uncovering. She broke my gaze to slip off my dress and I spun around to try to kiss her, to get her to the floor or the bed, both hidden in the dark, but it was too late. She saw my own tattoos clearly in the mirror, lit by that last gasp of light. Black coffins, identical, stacked up my spine. My back is slightly curved from scoliosis, but the coffin tattoos stack straight, pulling my body up with them. The one at the bottom is shown from the side, the lid partially off.

"I want to be able to look at you and look at them," she told me when I turned around and pressed my back into her body.

"You can't," I told her. "That's why they're on my back."

"Do you ever look at them?"

"No," I said. She knew it was a lie. "But I know where they are."

"Do you?"

She began tracing each one, starting from the nape of my neck and I imagined that the coffins were catching on fire and she was dipping her fingers into my burning skin. When she pushed me to the floor and twisted my hair around her fist until my face was turned as far back as it could be, only then did I realize I hadn't considered this position. That, on the floor, on my stomach, my neck craned, she could see both my eyes and the coffins.

6) How many personal mourners do you expect to attend the service?

    a) greater than 100
    b) 50-100
    c) 25-50
    d) 10-25
    e) 0-10
    f) 0

"I actually came here to ask you about a client," I said to Mónica.

"Which one?" Mónica asked the question easily, but something in her shifted. Though she didn't move, her body changed, became a scrap she had retreated from.

"The Connors. They called today—not to complain— but they mentioned that you'd stayed after the service?"

"I did," she said.

A further shift—her body unrecognizable before me.

"I don't know if that's a good idea." I wanted to touch her when I said this, but I didn't. "You've broken rules sometimes and that's been fine. This is a different level. A different breach."

She laughed, "Why?"

"We have to stay professional. There is a specific moment when our services end. If there isn't—" I stopped talking. Her hand was on my wrist. I didn't know how long it had been there. "The lines move. The roles blur. Our service becomes ill-defined."

"We could be mourning all the time," she said. She had worked her fingers tight around my arm and was moving them up slowly as if they were swallowing me.

"Yes," I said.

She smiled. "That's exactly what I want."

2) How are you connected to the deceased? Circle as many as apply.

Parent	Sibling	Friend (recently met) (life-long)		Business Partner
Spouse	Child	Partner	Lover	Family Member
Teacher	Student	Neighbor	Employer	Employee

Creative Collaborator   Member of religious/spiritual community

Other (please indicate):

Not personally connected to deceased

Many weeks later, when only three of my employees were still working, when I'd taken on all of their clients so that I was mourning several times a day, when I hadn't slept at home in a long time, Mónica woke up early for a service and asked me to go along. It was small, in an old Methodist church with mostly elderly attendants. I nodded to an old woman I knew in the pews. She'd been a client for years, had brought clients to me as well, a sort of unpaid ambassador.

We usually spoke when we met, but I just smiled at the old woman and her neat black hat, her black wool suit with a white rose. I tried to remember from her smile, the way she was sitting, what she filled out or recommended her friend fill out on the questionnaire. She always chose the questionnaire over the interview. She told me she loved the neatness, the way the questions seemed to approach pure action, ridding themselves of language. I knew she always checked somewhere between a *somber* and *moderate* grief display; she wanted a heartfelt demonstration, but a respectful one. *Respectful*, the only word of her own she allowed onto the page, penciled in each time as if I would forget.

We sat down in the pews and almost immediately, Mónica started to shake. No, *shake* is an inadequate word. What was happening was more like the warning tremors before an earthquake. The increasingly rapid movement of her legs made me reach for her despite my knowledge that she was receiving payment for her behavior. I put my hand on her leg and it was hot. I kept it there for as long as I could. Her keen had begun. The sound welled up from inside her as if filtered through broken stone. The wail rose. Mónica jumped from her seat. She climbed over the pew and burst through a row of folding chairs, running towards the open coffin.

I didn't look back at the old woman with the perfect hat and suit. I knew she hadn't asked for this. I knew without looking at her. But there was no way I could have looked at her. There was no possible existence in that moment except for Mónica, except for her grief.

She had reached the body—its slate gray coffin with gold details, the lily clasped between the old man's hands. She paused before it—the pause before her keen really began—and she inhaled as if inhaling the entire body, chipboard, gold enamel, white satin, lilies, cotton balls in the man's anus. We inhaled as well.

Mónica bent her knees and sprung onto the coffin. The woman in the black hat and black suit screamed. Men rushed to pull Mónica off. Her keen had started again, but no one was listening. She straddled the body, beating the man's chest with her fists, making hollow sounds that were somehow too audible.

At that moment I knew where all my employees had gone, where I was going too, where Mónica had led us. Everyone was looking at her, but I think only I saw it happen. Mónica paused—that intake between sound that removed everything from the air—and her fists stopped moving to rest on the dead man's sternum. She looked at his face and bent towards it slowly, reeling from the strain of her keen, the people pulling at her limbs.

I saw clearly, if only for an instant, like a single frame spliced into a film reel. I saw her hands, pressed hard on the man's chest. And then I couldn't see them. Where her palms and forearms had been was only the man's tweed suit and the art-deco wallpaper behind him. There was no outline of her fists, neither had she somehow sunk into the body. For an instant, a part of her had been completely erased.

III.

(el fantasma final)

THE BALLAD OF TAM LIN

Before the oyster folk took him from me, my father gave me his fiddle and told me the story it carried. On the island, he said, there were two sisters. I didn't know if he meant his island—cane and tobacco fields wracked by war—or Mam's—sea cliffs and highland meadows emptied by famine—or one of the many islands where he'd lived. The crowded island city where he met Mam. Or maybe an island he'd never even been to. My father held his fiddle up so that it seemed to hover in the air between us. Two sisters, he said, one dark-haired and the other one fair and they both fell in love with the miller's son.

I rolled my eyes. I hated stories about fair-haired sisters and miller's sons. My father cuffed my ear to make me listen. You'll like how this one goes, he told me. Both sisters loved the miller's son, but he had eyes for the fairer one. I scoffed again, but he just smiled. The smile that always made our audience—no matter what town we were in, how small, how ragged, how hungry they were for food other than flour and lard cakes—lean in and listen. The smile that told them he didn't care how side-eyed the townsfolk had first looked at him, at Mam and him together, at Mrs. Zhao leading her wagon, her daughter June behind her. The smile that said, if they just listened, if they just waited, he'd give them something as fine as stacks of cash-not-company-scrip, as the right amount of rain, as an answer to these hard times that wouldn't end. I waited for him, just like his smile told me to, just like every audience always did.

My father said the miller's son only wanted the fairer sister, so the dark-haired one went for a walk with her sister to the furthest point of their island. They passed palm groves and sea grape, walked until they were at the cliff's very edge. Then the dark-haired sister pushed the fair one over the cliff and down into the waves.

My father paused and raised his eyebrows, as if daring me to stop him, knowing I wouldn't now. Stories about miller's sons and fair sisters never went this way. The fair sister almost always died—on a riverbed or beneath a willow, run through by a saber, dropped by poison wine, or mad in an asylum like Cecilia Valdés—but never by her own sister's will. My father said the waves swept the fair sister out to sea. Fight as she did, clawing at water, kicking at waves, she sunk beneath the surface. The sea tugged her and carried her and stole her final breath. The sea pulled her deep. Sharks fed on her ribs, shrimp clung to her fingernails, until she was just a body, not a sister anymore and no longer fair.

Finally, the waves spit her back up. A wandering musician found her washed ashore and he didn't run away or call the priest or the mayor. The wanderer knelt down beside the mound of bones and hair.

My father asked me what I thought the wanderer did and I shook my head. I didn't know.

The wanderer picked up her finger bones, my father said, and he cut off her long, fair hair. He plucked her sternum from between her ribs and, because he was in need of it, he made a fiddle out of her. Her finger bones became the fiddle pegs, her hair the long bow strings, her white sternum the fiddle bridge.

Then my father handed me his fiddle, which he'd never before let me touch. We'd just crossed the border from Oregon to Washington, and were camped outside a logging town. The mud streets were empty, everyone deep in the woods sawing down cedar and sitka, the ground too wet for our wagons to move through and the rain too hard for even us to play a show in. I crouched on my bunk, tucked in a corner of our wagon. The rain beat down on the canvas tent above us, but it was warm inside. We'd start off again as soon as it was dry, searching for a town with people in it, though what kind of people and what they might ask of us, we never knew.

The pegs of my father's fiddle were deeply concaved, paper-thin in the middle and a pale yellow like old teeth, with hair-strand-wide dark cracks running over them. The bridge was the same color as the pegs, almost translucent in its delicacy. Since I could remember, I'd wanted to hold his fiddle: to trace the flor de mariposa and banana flowers carved across the back, to touch the wood stained almost black around the f-holes and deep red on the edges where it was constantly touched.

No matter what role he took in our show, my father always played his fiddle. He'd play a fast song at the beginning to rile up the crowd and a sad song at the end because everyone wants a lonesome ending. It brings the audience back again, hopeful they didn't remember right, that we'll give them the right ending the next time around. Though my father could play any instrument you could name, the fiddle was his favorite. But when he handed it to me in our muggy wagon—the horses chewing oats out of their feed box, Mam curled around him in their bunk, braiding the fringes on his jacket sleeve—I didn't question that I should get it. I had wanted it, had wanted the sound it made, the catch and pluck, its power to mold a crowd, to decide how well we would eat, how long we would stay by this mill or that farmstead. I had wanted the fiddle for what felt like an unimaginably long time. Back then, in our tent, steam rising off the horses and mixing with Mam's wordless hum, I would have used the word *forever*.

I didn't know how young I was. Didn't doubt what was owed me. Now, I wonder if my father gave me his fiddle because he knew something I didn't. If he had an idea of what would happen when we reached the oyster town we were headed towards. If he could scent some particular danger in the combination of mud, sea, and sawed cedar, and he gave me what mattered most to him. Offered me his fiddle for safe-keeping, heedless of my clumsy, too-small hands.

My father asked me what I thought the fiddle in the story sounded like. I was still holding his fiddle up in the air as he had handed it to me, not yet believing I could pull it close. When the wanderer first played the fiddle he'd made of the sister's bones and hair? What was the song? I couldn't speak, I shook my head again. Finally, I eased the fiddle down into my lap and traced its carvings: the flor de mariposa petals, the spider—intricate as a thousand I'd seen— perched on the flower's stem.

The fiddle sounded like the wind, my father said. The wind off the sea that carried the sister away, like the water dragging her under and spitting her back a heap of scraps, like the fishes that eat drowned girls. The fiddle sounded like the dark-haired one pushing her only sister off a cliff and the sound the dark-haired one made when she did what she thought she'd wanted and the sea carried her sister away. The fiddle sounded like the dark-haired sister's cruel heart, like her broken heart. Like the wind too, and like the rain that fell on her sister when she was only bones for a wanderer to comb through.

I nodded. He was right. That was how my father's fiddle sounded.

I don't have sisters or I have twenty. Our player's troupe was full of women who sometimes acted like my mother and sometimes like my friend. We cooked together, picked nettles and ferns and crab apples and kelp, swapped ribbons, wove ropes of cattails, patched the tents, gathered the horses when they spooked, faced down bears and wild cats, knowing when to run and when to stand still. I knew who made the best griddle cakes, who might slip honey into my clover tea, or let me sip her little-something-stronger and answer questions no one else would. My father's story couldn't make me afraid of these women, if that was what he tried at, these sisters and not sisters. Instead, I wondered, which part of the sister did the fiddle body come from? And what makes a man think bones make good fiddle pegs? I knew I was not like the sisters in the story. Or like the miller's son. I loved June Zhao and always would. Black is the color of my true love's hair.

I fell asleep with the fiddle in its case beside me. Just before dawn, we crossed a bridge over to a narrow peninsula and headed for the oyster town. A few gas lamps twinkled in the mountains behind us. Far out in the bay we could see the outline of ship masts and lighthouses, but the bridge itself was dark, like we'd been swallowed by a whale. For a moment, before the road dipped, we could see both the bay and the sea, the peninsula was so narrow. My father said we'd cook clams on the shore, that we'd fill our bellies whether

191

the oyster folk could pay for tickets or not. June was happy, talking of the shells she and Mrs. Zhao would clean and make into bracelets to sell, but Mam kept glancing back to the spot where we could see the open water through the line of sitkas. Mam was a strong swimmer, but she hated the sea. As she said, there was nothing out there to swim to.

I could already play the guitar and harmonica and our small accordion whose keys were mostly lost, but that the troupe kept for children to learn on. I could sing and accompany June on the washboard. If we'd had a piano, I bet I could have played that too, though we moved too often for the luxury. My father's rule was that everyone had to be able to carry what they owned and though we did have wagons with bunks and one for the sets and tools and junk you might not call junk when it fixes a wheel or plugs a tent's leaking roof, even the kids could carry everything they really needed to if they really needed to. If they needed to run. Not all troupes work this way, I've seen bands with trained bears and caged mountain cats, tables and chairs and stages sturdy enough to dance on, a whole line of extra wagons. But we ranged farther than most. I'd been born out east near Manhattan and here we were west again, for the second time I could remember, though farther west and north than we'd ever been. My father was oyster hunting, he said, that night he gave me his fiddle. He'd heard great crowds were to be found in the oyster towns, they'd pay you with coin because they had it and, unlike the fishing villages, they never strayed too far from home or lost half their population in a storm at sea. Oyster towns were places you could count on, places you could return to.

Light a troupe as we were, there was always a tension to my father and mother's bodies when we packed out of a town. No matter how many times we left, no matter that moving was our way of life, the tension never eased. Each morning when we packed out, Mam made sure we carried not an extra, unneedful scrap, no stones from rivers we forgot the names of, no town toys we'd traded for, no water turned fetid in our jugs. She would scour the tent on her hands and knees, shake our bedding, sweep out the dust, then empty her pack one more time and weigh each item in her hand, like the fates holding a life's string. Once the pack was finally clasped, she'd hitch it to her shoulder and glance behind her, though I doubt she knew herself just what she was looking for.

I thought nothing strange of waking always somewhere new, believed the jostle of the wagon beneath me the most natural way to fall asleep. But in some hidden part of themselves my parents treated every move like they were running. Not from the expected someones—church-, drink-, or hunger-mad locals—but from something older, buried so deep I don't think they ever saw the shadow's shape. Their worry was worn and palmed over, slipped to them by their parents at birth, without noticing, just as they had given it to me. Even now—grown as I am, with my own troupe to run—before I get anything new, whether it's barter or buy, I weigh what I might cast off in its place. I consider whether the addition of this shirt or cup, these extra nails, will make me lighter or easier to track. What small thing might be the difference between being able to leave and being forced to stay. I don't worry so much about the cost of an object as the weight.

We came to the oyster town in the middle of a harvest. Perhaps they were always harvesting. Mounds of shells, huge as houses, lined the road leading to the town and children climbed up them, the shells skidding out from under their bare feet, their knees scabbed from barnacles. The tide was out and the bay was covered with men bent half over, holding long rakes for stealing oysters from their beds. They scraped the oysters into open baskets and the women lugged the baskets to the shore when they were full. The more I looked, the more mounds appeared. Their outlines, scattered and blurred by the children's feet, crept closer and closer to the road.

June and me and Sam—our blacksmith Cordero's youngest brother—dug clams, chasing bubbles of air through the cold, shallow water and digging into the silty mud until we couldn't feel our fingers. We steamed the clams over the campfire, with sea asparagus and purple laver pulled off the rocks, briny enough that we needed no butter or salt. The clams were still filled with silt, their bellies green with mustard so we ate them slowly in the peninsula's long twilight, spitting out the sand when enough collected under our tongues. Mrs. Zhao said she'd soak the rest overnight with a handful of cornmeal to clean them. Clams again tomorrow, she promised, and no sand between our teeth.

We would do *The Ballad of Tam Lin* for the oyster town. The show required complex costume changes and contained some of our most daring scenes. I wasn't yet ready to play the fiddle though I'd practiced all day. In the afternoon, Mrs. Zhao kicked me out of the shadow of their tent, shooing me away with her arms lifted over her head until I was out on the sand flats, and far enough from the tents to play freely. By then the patch under my chin where the fiddle rested was rubbed raw. I petted the patch, same as my father's, knowing I'd have it all my life. Seagulls dove in among the beds, unafraid of shovels or shouts. On the shore, women scrubbed the shells, shucking some, leaving others whole. The mounds of shells seemed bigger than when we arrived and I wondered if maybe they had swallowed houses, if there was a whole other town beneath them, hollowed out and consumed, or sleeping, about to wake.

That night I would be back on the guitar and singing, June on the washboard, her tin-capped gloves flashing in the torches we'd set in the dune grass. Mrs. Zhao would play Janet, who runs from her castle to the moor of Carterhaugh, picks a red rose, and accidentally summons Tam Lin, the wild shade. Mam, in her long red coat and a wand of pine branches thick with cobwebs and silvery moss, would play the fairy queen. And my father, of course, would play Tam Lin, roaring like a bear, growling like a lion, changing before the audience's eyes into unimaginable shapes.

In the New England towns bright with white-walled churches and clean-swept barns, we kept the story simple— Janet a maid who saves her betrothed with a hero's task. But out on the peninsula, between the bay and the sea, we were far from those churches, those necks still stiff from their great-great-great grandfathers' pilgrim collars. In the oyster town, we told the whole story: Tam Lin laying Janet down in the roses; Janet walking the castle halls, her face green as glass from puking her guts out each morning; Janet back on the moor in search of a poison rose, the special bitter root. We never said the poison was to kick the baby out of her, but the oyster folk knew it and their faces tightened at that verse, wan as Janet's when she learns she's carrying a baby from a wild shade.

But their faces relaxed a little when Tam Lin pulls Janet from the dirt and thorn. When he promises that if she can hold him tight through the fairy queen's spells, he'll transform into a gentleman. The fairy queen turns Tam Lin into a lion, a bear, finally a blazing iron rod, and it is only then that Janet can pick him up and throw him in the well. He emerges from the water, naked and free.

On the sand before the oyster folk, my father growled and thrashed in Mrs. Zhao's arms and Sam and Cordero leapt up to make the changes to his costume, the lion's mane, the tiger's tale, the iron's flame, the well's water, until Tam Lin is weeping on the ground and Janet covers him in her cloak and brings him home. When my father landed on the hard-packed sand, plain and only a man, the oyster men cheered, crossed the invisible line we'd made to mark our stage, and raised my father into the air. We sang the final verse with him perched on their shoulders, the oyster women circling behind them, peering over their husbands' backs at my father, the cowrie bead necklaces he always wore visible on his bare chest, his costumes forgotten on the sand. The women held back, their hands over their cheeks to hide their blushes, until we'd all had oyster stew and beer brewed dark with shells. Then the wives, pink-cheeked, stroked the bear skin Tam Lin threw off and the silk fairy wings Mam still wore laced around her shoulders. The children warmed to us last, though they were usually first, and when they finally approached us, they wanted not to see the costumes, but our instruments.

June showed off her drums and washboard, then clipped her harmonica to the washboard so she could play both at once while I sang. Sam kept his eyes on the oyster kids, mindful they didn't go in our tents or touch anything we couldn't fix. But I had just been given the fiddle and my fingers twitched for the dark red wood and how it warmed in my hands, the smell of the resin rising off the bow when I played. I knew I shouldn't, but I snuck into my tent and brought out the fiddle. The rest of the troupe was back on the packed sand of our stage, around the fire where we'd steamed clams. Mam and Mrs. Zhao were singing and my father had his accordion and I could hear each of their particular voices until Mrs. Zhao chose a song the oyster folk could sing and they all joined in, their voices heaving and tossing, overwhelming the ones I knew, an unruly chorus rising up into the night.

I strummed my fiddle and the children all turned towards me, their faces scrubbed to attend the show, their clothes and hands and mine smelling of the sea and bay mud. A wind carried over the water and I knew there were whales out beyond the bay, their song rolling through the cold, flipping ocean liners by accident or rage. We stood on the furthest point of land, no islands between them and us and the endless sea. The wind carried the acrid scent of the paper mills from across the bridge, the wind twanged the fiddle strings, whistling through the taut belly, and the fiddle did seem made of bones, it did cry out. I told the oyster kids the story my father had told me and I sang the song of Geordie, who is accused of killing the king's wild deer and whose wife begs in front of the judge to keep him from the noose. I sang of the ghosts who roamed jungles in search of guayaba fruit, who were just like the rest of us in every way except they had no navel, and June joined in, she loved ghost songs. One boy, his hair shaved close, scalp nicked with scabbed-over cuts, crept closer and closer to me, like he wanted to steal inside the f-holes and sleep in my fiddle's belly. At the campfire, my father laughed his seal-bark laugh and growled to scare the oyster wives and Mam shrieked at him to stop. I tried to spot their outlines in the crowd. The boy came closer, until I could barely move my arm and bow to play, and then he punched me in the stomach, grabbed the fiddle, dove behind a clump of marsh grass, and disappeared.

Sam and June both raced after the thief, but I couldn't move. We knew how to fight and we knew how to run, but a fiddle could be smashed and I'd only just been given mine. Mam's and Mrs. Zhao's voices rose above the wind, they were singing Geordie's song now too, the oyster folk quiet to listen. The king won't be swayed by Geordie's wife, no matter how she prays, no matter how many children she has. My father sang the final verse alone. What he'd do to me if the fiddle was crushed. So, I ran too, though I'd waited too long, though I didn't know which direction I was headed, though both Sam and June were lost to the dark.

My father used to run away from our troupe. Not in the way others left—by picking up with someone other than who they joined with, or staying when we moved on, or never coming back to their wagons. He would really run. Usually, it was once we'd stopped for the night, on a riverside or crossroads, when the tents were pitched and the campfires made, the scent of wood smoke, frying onions, and clothes drying making the spot seem ours. He'd look up from the fire and just tear away from us, like he'd seen a bear or an approaching army. He'd growl and roar and wrench at his hair, like he was playing Tam Lin. No one could hold him. Sometimes he'd run towards a farmstead, steal horses from lonely pastures, pluck cooling pies off of porches. Sometimes he'd leap from the wagon while we were still moving. He'd land in the hard dirt and run as fast as he could away from us. He broke two ribs once that way.

I'd always be sent to find him and I'd take June and Sam to help coax him home, their faces slack to remind him he was running from nothing so frightening, their hands outstretched and cupped like they carried scraps for a stray dog. It might take him hours to stop running and we couldn't speak to him until he'd stopped, though lucky for me he never ran anywhere straight. The path he left was easy to follow too, like a wild boar's, tearing through the grass and brambles, breaking branches and whipping saplings—if he had claws, he'd have scraped up the trees and dirt, marking the forest around him. We never spoke of his running or tried to explain it and it wasn't connected to drink or fighting with Mam or me pestering him. But I got so I could feel the run building in him, got to trust and believe the preceding signs, his hands fluttering at his side like hummingbird wings, his laugh faint and compressed, so unlike his usual untamed bark. No use trying to keep him when he started fluttering, there was only following his trail and leading him back home, his clothes torn, hands and neck scratched, shame-faced, but finally stilled.

He never spoke of his running. But from the stories he told of the Armando Castells—his long-lost family strewn across tiny islands and vast continents—I came to believe it was inherited, this peeling off, this disappearing, this fleeing from something no one else could see.

Once, after I found him and he'd calmed, he offered me a stolen roast, the skin black and crisp, snatched from some farmer's summer cellar. He carefully picked off the leaves and dirt from where he'd dropped it in his chase and held it up for me. I peeled off a bite and he smiled then, broad and clean, the smile of him returned to us. We ate the roast for several days.

But if I couldn't find him, Mam would start packing the wagon, even if we had only just set up camp. She'd fix the horses back into their yoke, climb on the spring seat, and twitch the reins. Once all the trunks and bundles were packed, once Mam had stopped looking around and only faced forward in the opposite direction from where we'd come, only then did my father appear out of the trees, panting and wild-eyed, back to catch us before we left.

Out of the campfire's glow, I could see more of the peninsula and the outskirts of the oyster town. The stars stretched over the water and there was no separating their lights from the lights of the few houses across the bay. But if I turned away from them, the marsh grass appeared out of the black, and the mountains of oyster shells sent up a faint white glow. No sounds from June or Sam, they were too far to hear or they were listening like me, knowing the fiddle thief would know where to hide, would know the land better than us. What he didn't know was that June and me could see in the dark, and Sam, Sam could hear what only deer and dogs could.

I took a clipped-grass road, carved between dune grass and sword fern, the ground soggy and puckered behind the line of houses, and finding nothing, followed the dark back out to the sand. But the path dipped into the marsh, and the horizon—at least where I guessed it was—disappeared. I could have been anywhere, any state, any shore, whether lake or sea, or at the edge of a river rushing just deep enough to carry me away. The hard-packed sand gave way to soft dunes, and a huge shape rose out of what I thought was solid land. A bear, hulking and rank, smelling not just of the sea, but musk and gore. The bear stared in my direction, snout tilted upward, sniffing the air. I froze, but the bear settled again into the sand, its form folding back into the dune's shadows. Once the bear was still, and making sleepy, smacking noises with its tongue, I backed away, sticky flowers and sea asparagus crunching beneath my feet. I walked until I could see the campfire again, in the opposite direction I thought it'd be.

The firelight dipped and hid, crowded out by the bodies dancing and swaying around it, the music drowned by shouts. That time of night when someone in the troupe—did they draw straws for this task as we do now?—broke from the crowd and rounded the children up and carried us to our wagons, or an empty wagon at least, if ours was in use. Usually, Mrs. Zhao or Mam or Nestor who cooked and took care of the horses, someone, though rarely my father, would step away from the fire and search for us. Or perhaps we'd been forgotten, as we sometimes were, and then we stayed up with the fire and stars and laughed at how all town folk looked the same sleeping over each other in the open air, the morning sun burning the miners' and factory workers' noses alike.

I kept my eyes on the capricious light, moving closer to the lone willow growing out of the sand, its branches snarled by the wind, salt scorched on the western side. I thought I could climb the willow and, maybe from its branches, see the fiddle thief or June or Sam. I was watching the branches, planning how I'd climb them, scared of what more I might find in the shadows, not looking at the ground when I tripped. I fell, my hands splayed, not onto dune grass or sand, but onto a body, a body curled around the willow trunk.

I didn't know at first that the body was a her, thought maybe I'd tripped over another bear and woken it, and I was dead this time for sure, but the body was past waking. I turned her over and her face was pale like Janet's, like the fiddle sister, like the six maids the cruel youth drowns in the sea. I touched her face and she wasn't anyone I knew, the smell of oysters, her cheek soft, but my hand came back wet with still-warm blood.

Years later, I learned that the story of the fiddle sister was much older than my father, much older than even his fiddle. It was a song from my mother's island though my father told the story like it was from his own. Sure, Mam said, years after the oyster town, when she was crooked and hoarse and no longer played the fairy queen, I sang you that for years. Don't you remember?

There are many versions. Sometimes the sisters are from the country, sometimes from a city in Tennessee we've passed many times. Sometimes, the fiddle sister sings not just the wind and the rain, but the truth, and she saves the falsely accused from certain hanging. Sometimes, now, I play the miller's son. But I know I am all of the characters: the wanderer picking up the fiddle from the sand, the body whittled to bones, and most of all the dark-haired sister, pushing the one she loved most into the crashing waves.

June found me beside the willow tree and pulled me away from the body circled around it. I don't know how long I'd crouched there, but by the time June took my hand, the blood where I'd smeared it across my jacket had begun to crackle and rust dry. June brought me away from the body, her hand in mine, the other holding the fiddle. We kept the bay to one side, the marsh to the other, until I started shaking, hard, and couldn't stand the feel of those dirty clothes against my skin, until I begged her to get them off me, to get them away from me. And she listened. She must have done what we never did, throw my clothes out, toss them in the water or bury them in the sand, because I didn't see them again, not as rags or quilt patches or stitched into one of the costumes. They never resurfaced.

Mrs. Zhao's wagon was empty and we crawled into June's bunk, legs stiff from the cold. June had fought the thief and won the fiddle back. The bow hairs were split, a peg lost in the sand, but the body was whole. The long neck uncracked. I couldn't find the bridge, June said, I looked, and I told her it was fine, we would search again once it was light. I was sure we would stay in the oyster town for a few days at least, do a longer show, begin a story that would make them wonder when we'd come back, and they'd repeat the songs we'd sung amongst themselves until we returned.

Beneath June's blankets damp from sea spray, I whispered all the songs I knew: Geordie, Tam Lin, Cecilia Valdés, though I didn't let myself imagine how my fingers would spread across the fiddle or the ache of the chin rest against my skin.

June was silent while I whispered the words to the songs. It was as if the body I'd found by the willow tree was a ghost without a navel and it had cast its spell over us, making us pliant and quiet. I never faulted June for not asking what I'd seen in the cove by the willow tree, for sneaking us back to the wagons without speaking to anyone, for slipping with me under a spell of silence. I like to think that if she'd known what our silence would bring, she would have made me speak, and if I'd spoken, I'd have learned what we were leaving behind. I like to think I would never have let us leave.

Mrs. Zhao always packed the opposite of Mam. She pushed whatever spilled from her wagon back in, sorted nothing, not caring what scraps or strays she picked up from the sand. June packs now the same as her mother did. Everywhere we go, June collects everything she can. Owl feathers and robin eggs, the remnants of a red-striped china dinner set, but she prefers anything that sparkles, even if it's only in the rain or a certain light. If I was to tell the story of how I won her—like how Willie of Wainsbury won Jane while her father the king was long in Spain, or how Leonardo de Gamboa wooed Cecilia Valdés through her balcony grate—I'd tell of what I'd given June: a hummingbird's nest of horsehair, a Luna moth's lost wing, my skirt full over and again with pawpaws and serviceberries and morels. In the troupe, people come and go: before the oyster folk, Mam stayed a whole summer in a silk mill town, I later learned with the foreman there, even Sam eventually strayed too, helped a family in Utah with haying and, tired of always leaving, stayed with them at their big pine table. But June was born into the troupe, just like me. There's no memory I have that she's not in or on the edge of, about to enter and set me trembling. Stories are about change and me and June isn't much of a story. She's beside me, always arriving, never gone.

June and I woke to the sound of the wagon wheels clattering over the bridge slats, the light bouncing off the water far below and illuminating patches of the tent tarp above us. I ran alongside the wagons, past Sam and Cordero's, Nestor and Dolores's, to ours at the front of the line. I climbed into our wagon and tucked the fiddle beneath my blankets, hoping I could hide it from my father until I could make a new bridge, repair the bow, polish the wood. Mam sat alone on the wagon's spring seat. Our horses could wade through rivers and swim while the wagon floated behind them, but they hated crossing high above water, so Mam kept the reins tight, leading the horses through their fear. She was still wearing her red fairy queen coat, the wool so thin in some places that the white inner webbing showed through, the hem so dark with grime it looked soaked in salt water. She didn't speak to me when I joined her on the seat, she kept her hands on the reins, even after we had crossed the bridge and were back on the highroad and the horses hardly needed leading.

I didn't worry that my father wasn't sitting beside her. If he had been running or drinking, Mam might make him sleep in the set tent, where there was no bunk and the tools rattled without wool or blankets to batten them. But he was always near us, leading the horses or curled up behind a trunk, his solid body tucked somewhere in our long line of wagons. No matter how far off he'd run, we always waited for him. Mam might get ready, might *make* like she was going, but only to draw him back to her. She'd never actually left without him. To do so would be like stepping alone into the sea.

What I didn't know then, sitting by Mam, was that the oyster folk had grabbed my father just before dawn, while June and I were asleep in her bunk. They locked him up for killing the girl I'd found beneath the willow, though he'd been almost the whole night by the campfire singing and playing his accordion and dancing with the oyster women and even the oyster men when they'd had enough to drink to do what they wanted, his teeth flashing in the firelight, his black beard pointed to the sky, his black hair loose and wild. How long does it take to kill a girl? the oyster folk asked. Could have been done pretty quick, in the time he took to go off in search of the children, slip away and back to keep dancing, smiling all the while, an accent he didn't have layered on him in their telling. They'd seen him turn into a bear and a lion and they'd heard him growl and shake. Who could hold him? Who could stop him?

My father told Mam he'd follow after us, said they held him on a song. He told her, don't look back and he'd be coming with.

You might ask why Mam didn't stay with my father? Why she didn't ask Mrs. Zhao to keep a watch on me while she fought to get him out of that tiny jail cell beneath the church? Why she didn't beg the whole troupe to stay until he was back with us?

When we'd first crossed the bridge the day before, look-ing for oyster towns, she'd kept flicking her eyes towards the shore, towards the salt-stripped trees that parceled out the view of the open water. But unlike then—before we'd eaten the sandy clams, before I'd stumbled in the dark be-side the willow, before the bear, the body of the girl—when we crossed the bridge without my father, Mam didn't look back to the water or to the road we'd come on. She didn't wait for sunrise, for an extra hour. You might call her cruel and unfaithful, but you forget Mam knew the songs she sang well. Mam knew that though Geordie's wife handed out a hundred coins to the poor folk at court and asked them each to pray, though she told the judge of her six children, though she said if the judge were in the square outside the court and she armed with pistol and saber she'd fight him herself, still her Geordie hung from a silver chain and his wife left without her coins, back to her six children, the sev-enth lying in her body.

Though I didn't see her do it, I know that before I woke that morning, when I was still curled next to June, Mam picked up her bag and weighed it. She decided, in the shadow of the tent, what she could carry away and what had to be left. She'd made her pack and mine too, as light as they could be.

I patched my father's fiddle poorly and then patched it again, better each time. For years, I believed my father's words, believed we'd find him again, or he'd find us, and he'd ask me to play the fiddle and sing him all I'd seen since the oyster town. I'd tell him then that I was sorry I didn't save him, didn't even know to try. Sorry I slept curled around June while the mob stole him from us. Sorry I lost my fid-dle and he had to stray so far from the beach in search of me. For years, I believed I'd seen another figure between the bear and the willow tree, silhouetted against the shadows. Something scrawny, two-legged, and too tall to be the fiddle thief. An oyster man, far from the crowd, picking his way through the dark. Some nights I thought it was him I'd seen, not a bear at all. And I'd tell my father I was sorry for telling no one about this oyster man, for remembering him only long after we'd crossed the bridge, for growling and thrashing against Mam when it was too late, when we were days gone, for maybe not seeing him at all. But I figure now that my father's command to not look back was probably not even his, just some words Mam told me to keep me silent and still, keep me on the wagon seat beside her.

Not too long ago, in Santa Fe, I was able to get a bridge of white bone for my father's fiddle. I can play like no one else. There isn't a song I can't learn if I want to, but my fiddle I save for the songs that sound like wind and rain, like the weeping Mam never did in my hearing, like burying Mrs. Zhao in winter after her cough wouldn't stop, like forgetting my father's roar because we kept playing Tam Lin though he wasn't there and new players sang in his place. I moved to the front of the show and so did June. I keep my hair short and bind my chest so I can play Willie of Wainsbury and Leonardo de Gamboa and Tam Lin too and June plays Jane and Cecilia Valdés and Janet. And I sing the song my father used to, of a woman in his family, a woman who rose out of the sea, her body made of emerald water and night sky, who wooed a foreign conqueror and bent him to her will. We end each night with a song on my father's fiddle, June's voice rising with my bow and echoing in the dark red wood, the carvings of flor de mariposa and banana flowers fainter now, but still there. We know the songs well, we know Geordie hangs, Leonardo de Gamboa is killed, Cecilia Valdés dies alone in an asylum, her daughter lost to her. But for a moment when we play, when June's voice twists my fiddle pegs into tune, when the song takes us into the dark, to the distance between stars, to the moon looking back at us, seeing us, deep into the sea among whales and wrecked ships, into that space beyond words, beyond our bodies, beyond even the song, for a moment we are as gullible as the town folk who stay put and listen. I believe my father's words again, believe he'll be waiting in the next town, come out of the next woods, and want to hear me play. I look at June and, fools that we are, I know what we're both thinking. That the song might change, a different ending might appear, and we chase a verse that's never been sung, shaped though it is by the wind and the rain and all the other old forces, a story we still don't know yet.

NOTES

"Ana Mendieta Haunts The Block" draws on the artworks of Ana Mendieta and Donald Judd. The story fictionalizes Mendieta and Judd's lives. Thank you to the helpful and informative guides at The Block at Marfa, a fabulous museum. Thank you to Ana Mendieta, eternal.

Thank you to Magdalena Zurawski for telling me the true story which "The Burial of Fidelia Armando Castell" grew from.

"Palm Chess" draws on the imagery, techniques, and writing of Maya Deren.

At a party many years ago, someone told me the story of a dream they had about a magical elephant's foot. I wish I could remember who, so I could thank you and give you credit.

"Are We Ever Our Own" draws on the artwork and writings of Hannah Wilke, Donald Judd, Adrian Piper, Paul Thek, Robert Irwin, and Lee Bontecou.

"Mr. A & Company" draws on the Tide Jewels stories and the works of Kazuo Ohno.

"The Ballad of Tam Lin" includes references to the Child Ballad of the same name, and draws on "The Twa Sisters," "Black is the color of my true love's hair," *Cuban Legends* by Salvador Bueno, *Running in the Family* by Michael Ondaatje,

Anaïs Mitchell's albums *Hadestown* and *Child Ballads*, and *Cecilia Valdés* by Cirilo Villaverde.

For those who do not know her, La Virgen de la Caridad del Cobre, the patron saint of Cuba, is a syncretism of Atabey, Our Lady of Illescas, and Oshun. She is all of these at once and something else as well.

ACKNOWLEDGMENTS

Thank you to the editors of the following publications in which these stories, often in different forms, first appeared:

The Common: "Ana Mendieta Haunts The Block";
The New England Review: "The Burial of Fidelia Armando Castell";
Cosmonauts Avenue: "Two-Gallon Heart";
Big Fiction: "The Night of the Almiqui";
One Story: "The Elephant's Foot";
Slice Magazine: "Are We Ever Our Own";
Strange Horizon: "Palm Chess";
Western Humanities Review: "Mr. A and Company";
The Coffin Factory: "The Field of Professional Mourning."

Image on contents page, *Solenodon cubanus (Atopogale cubana)* by Monika Bentley. Copyright released to public domain.

Thank you to the early readers of these stories, especially: my workshops in Boulder and Athens, Elisabeth Sheffield, Jeffrey DeShell, Stephen Graham Jones, Magdalena Zurawski, and Reginald McKnight.

A special thanks to Danielle Bukowski for her support of my work.

Thank you to Vera Kurian, Everdeen Mason, Ali Sharman, and Melissa Silverman for letting me join your writers group, for reading my work, for your thoughtful notes, and for your friendship.

Thank you to the University of Colorado-Boulder, the University of Georgia, and the University of Maryland for the funding and support I received while writing these stories.

I have been extremely lucky to receive support from the following residencies. Thank you for the gift of time and community: Anderson Center, Blue Mountain Center, Yaddo, Hedgebrook, Willapa Bay Artist Residency, the Millay Colony, Lighthouse Works.

Thank you to Federico García Lorca, whose words are interwoven throughout my first novel.

Thank you to my dear friends, to the ladies of 168 Williams. A special thank you to Jason for convincing me to finish this book.

Thank you to my parents, with all my love.

And thank you to my dearest Thibault, always my first and last reader, always by my side.

A deep bow to my ancestors, who I hope to remember and honor in these pages.

ABOUT THE AUTHOR

Gabrielle Lucille Fuentes is the author of *The Sleeping World* (Touchstone-Simon & Schuster). She has received fellowships from Hedgebrook, Willapa Bay Artists in Residency, Yaddo, the Millay Colony, Lighthouse Works, Anderson Center, and the Blue Mountain Center. Her work has appeared in *New England Review*, *The Common*, *One Story*, *Cosmonauts Avenue*, *Slice*, *Pank*, *NANO Fiction*, *Western Humanities Review*, and elsewhere. She holds a BA from Brown University, an MFA from the University of Colorado, Boulder, and a PhD from the University of Georgia. She is an Assistant Professor at the University of Maryland, where she teaches creative writing and Latinx literature.

BOA Editions, Ltd. American Reader Series

Colophon

BOA Editions, Ltd., a not-for-profit publisher of poetry and other literary works, fosters readership and appreciation of contemporary literature. By identifying, cultivating, and publishing both new and established poets and selecting authors of unique literary talent, BOA brings high-quality literature to the public. Support for this effort comes from the sale of its publications, grant funding, and private donations.

The publication of this book is made possible, in part, by the special support of the following individuals:

Anonymous
June C. Baker
Christopher C. Dahl, *in memory of J. D. McClatchy*
Joseph Finetti & Maria Mastrosimone
Elizabeth Forbes & Romolo Celli,
in memory of Surresa & Richard Forbes
Robert L. Giron
James Long Hale
Margaret Heminway
Nora A. Jones
Paul LaFerriere & Dorrie Parini
John & Barbara Lovenheim
Joe McElveney
Boo Poulin
Deborah Ronnen
David W. Ryon
Meredith & Adam Smith,
in memory of Mary Margaret Stewart
William Waddell & Linda Rubel
Glenn & Helen William